Discover for yourself why readers can't get enough of the multiple award-winning publisher, Ellora's Cave. Whether you prefer e-books or paperbacks, be sure to visit EC on the web at www.ellorascave.com for an erotic reading experience that will leave you breathless.

www.ellorascave.com

Ellora's Cave Publishing, Inc.
1337 Commerce Dr. #13
Stow, OH 44224

ISBN # 1-4199-5127-0

Edited by Cris Brashear.
Cover art by Darrell King.

Warning: The following material contains strong sexual content
meant for mature readers. *The Best of Jaid Black* has been rated E,
erotic, by a minimum of three independent reviewers. We
strongly suggest storing this book in a place where young
readers not meant to view it are unlikely to happen upon it. That
said, enjoy…

THE BEST OF
JAID BLACK

A collection of three Jaid Black novellas
never before in paperback

TREMORS

To Fredrik, and happy endings…

Part I:
The Hunt

Chapter 1
Göthmoor, Sweden
Present Day

Pulling the black cloak more securely around her body, Marie Robb alighted from her rental car and into the chilled night air. Her nipples hardened instantly as the cold, moaning wind seeped through the cloth of the woolen garment and permeated the single layer of the silk evening gown she wore beneath it. Throwing a long honey-colored tress over her shoulder, she visually scanned the area to either side of the dirt road.

"Great," she sighed. "Just great. There's nothing around here for miles."

Rubbing her arms briskly to ward off the chill bumps quickly forming on her flesh, she took a deep breath and blindly looked out into the night, her gaze flicking across the desolate dirt road her Saab had just sacrificed a tire to. "Dad always said never take the back roads." She sighed again. "But do I ever listen? No way."

Kicking the deflated Saab tire with the toe of her stiletto pump, she frowned as she thrust her hands to her hips in frustration. Of all the times not to have heeded her father's advice, Marie thought, why did she have to go and do it while traveling in a foreign country?

Shaking her head, she opened the passenger door to the Saab, gathered up her purse, and slammed the door shut behind her. The sound reverberated into the dark night and through the forest trees that surrounded her on either side, underlining the fact that she was indeed in the middle of nowhere. Chills raced up and down the length of her spine as Marie considered for the first time just how alone she was. Alone and without any manner of protection.

She swallowed roughly. Suddenly she wished she'd heeded more of her father's advice. Namely that she'd actually showed up to those self-defense classes he'd enrolled her into.

Chastising herself for allowing her overactive imagination to get the better of her, she straightened her spine, took a deep breath, and determined to find a path that would lead to…anywhere.

Besides, she thought, she could take care of herself. She had come to Europe to find herself, to grow up and make her own way in life. She hadn't come here to convince herself that her father was always right and that she'd be better off marrying a doctor, bearing a couple of children, and living in a house with a white picket fence smack-dab in the middle of *Green Acres*. That was her father's idea of happiness, not hers.

And this place, she told herself as her gaze flicked warily about, was most definitely not *Green Acres*. More like The Haunted Forest from *The Wizard of Oz*.

The wind began to moan, inducing a few new chill bumps to course down her spine. The sounds of unknown forest creatures grew prominent as she noticed them for the first time. A rodent of some sort scampered by, causing her to yelp.

This, she decided on a frown, was definitely not what she'd had in mind when she'd flown to Europe to experience new things.

Biting her lip, Marie scanned the area once more, trying to find a path she could traverse that would lead her to some sort of help. Her gaze darted north, south, east, west, and—nothing, she sighed.

She'd almost given up entirely when, a minute later, a faint moonbeam spilled over an area of the forest, highlighting a barely worn but definite path that led into it. Her eyebrows rose.

She stilled, considering the fact that she had no makeshift light to take with her into the forest, yet she would still have to enter it. There was no aid to be found on this abandoned dirt road she was standing in the middle of.

Ignoring the wind that whipped the heavy black cloak about her, Marie threw her purse over her shoulder and resigned herself to the inevitable. She would take the path. She had to. There was no other choice.

Her heart rate picking up exponentially, she walked slowly toward her destination. Every step felt heavy and methodical, as if an unseen force had somehow zeroed in on her and was pulling her into its midst.

She mentally rolled her eyes at her dramatic thoughts. She should have been an actress.

She felt tired when she finally made her way to the edge of the dirt road, like she'd walked ten miles instead of ten paces. Shaking off the bizarre feeling, she stepped onto the grassy terrain that led into the gut of the forest. Her costly designer heels sunk into the muddy earth, bringing her height back down to its true five feet and six inches.

Taking a deep breath, Marie stared wide-eyed down the narrow path for as far as the eye could see. It didn't escape her notice that she couldn't see very far down it, and that there was no telling how deep into the woods it went...or where it might lead to.

It was the last thought that made her shiver, a condition that seemed to worsen with each bogged down step she took. "Well, Marie," she muttered under her breath, "at least you haven't bumped into Count Dracula yet."

A bat swooped down, hovering over her head for an extended moment before disappearing into the thick of the black woods. Her green eyes rounding, Marie half-snorted and half-laughed. "Damn," she breathed out, "I better quit mumbling. Everything I say seems to be coming true."

Reaching out in front of her, she lifted up the arm of a low-hanging branch and moved to the other side of it. The branch slammed down behind her, enveloping her into the heart of the path. Muttering something incoherent about her father and where was the old bastard when she needed him, Marie shook off her misgivings and continued down the path once again.

The crisp wind whipped the black wool cloak about her legs, parting it on one side and revealing the slit the slinky black evening gown made to her upper thigh. The barrette she wore in her hair came undone, causing long golden locks to spill from it and cascade down around her waist. Marie absently drew the hood of the cloak up and around her head, not thinking twice about the black barrette now laying discarded and forgotten in the muddied path.

The trail was so barely traversed that it was hard to make out where she should and shouldn't walk, but a faint sprinkle of moonlight continued to trickle down through the trees, illuminating the path just enough to enable her to go on.

For miles Marie walked, each tree having the same appearance as the last, every step taking her further and deeper into the forest's lair. She was tired, so incredibly exhausted. Every bone in her body seemed to ache, reminding her of how stupid she'd been to drive the Saab down a back road in a country she'd been in for all of two days.

And all because of *him*. The stranger. That mysterious man she'd met just a few hours past at the opening of the Göthmoor Museum's exhibit on ancient cultures.

He had insisted that this was a good way to come. He had claimed that he'd driven the dirt road several times en route to his estate and that it was a reliable shortcut. And Marie, naïve fool that she now realized she was, had believed him.

And why had she taken him at his word? she asked herself for the hundredth time in the past few hours. Why, when everything about the stranger had sent little danger signals jolting through her body?

Panting heavily for lack of air, Marie sank to the ground of the forest, not caring that her cloak became muddied in the process. Closing her eyes and breathing deeply, she scooted up against the bark of a tree and considered the answer to her own question. She knew the answer already, of course. She would have to be incredibly stupid not to.

She had wanted, quite simply, to escape the stranger's unnerving presence. She would have done anything, gone anywhere, taken any supposed shortcut in creation, to put as much distance between him and her as possible, and as quickly as possible.

Even now in her mind's eye she could see the man's tall, brooding form hovering over her. When she closed her eyes like this it wasn't difficult to visualize the harshness of his austere features, the black of his short cropped hair contrasted against silver at the temples, the icy blue of his eyes…and the way those eyes had undressed her, piece by methodical piece, throughout the course of the evening.

Marie had felt the stranger's gaze on her at all times. Whether meeting her eyes dead on or boring a hole into the back of her skull as she made her way by each displayed piece of the exhibit, she had felt the possessiveness in his wolf's eyes clear down to her toes.

The knowledge of it had frightened her, and just as terrifyingly, it had also induced tremors of desire to curl up in her belly. She had never been the type to want a man at first glance. Especially not a stranger so mysterious, and if one listened to village gossip, so evil as well.

It was those eyes, those damn eyes, she decided. The same clear blue predator's gaze that had undressed her body as though he owned it. The same wolf's eyes that had mesmerized her as he'd come to a halt before her and made his intentions known.

"You will belong to me," he stated simply, matter-of-factly, in a deep rich voice whose English was heavily accented.

Marie's large green eyes widened. "I-I don't know what you mean," she blithered out dumbly, not knowing what else to say.

He was strange, she thought. Men didn't just walk up to women and say things like that.

She blinked. "I will belong to no one but myself."

His eyes roamed down the length of her then, leaving her face and settling on her cleavage. One side of his mouth lifted in a slight smile.

"I-I need to go," she breathed out. Good lord, the man was bizarre. Like a recluse who rarely came into contact with others, he seemed to have no social manners at all. The image of a wild animal let loose at a formal ceremony filled her mind. "I have to go back to the hotel now." With great effort, she broke his gaze and began to back away from him.

As a reply, he merely nodded his head, his gaze considering her every movement. "You are staying at Göthmoor's one and only inn, I presume?"

She didn't answer him. Rude or not, her only thought was to be away from him. He was strange. Frightening.

"There's a dirt road behind the museum," he quietly called out, unaffected by the fact that she'd just given him the cold shoulder. *"It's a shortcut. I use it myself. It will take you home."*

Home, Marie thought morosely, coming back to the present. Her eyes flicked about the forest. She'd give anything to be back home in the States this very moment, snuggled up with a book, her favorite blanket draped across her lap.

The bark of the tree began to chafe the skin on her back, reminding her once again that she'd walked for miles and still had not encountered a single soul. The totality of her predicament became horrifyingly apparent. Had he done this to her on purpose? Had the stranger been affected by her dismissal of him and seen to it that he'd gained some manner of revenge over her?

Marie rolled her eyes at her dramatic thoughts. How could he have known that the Saab would get a flat tire out in the middle of nowhere? No man, regardless to how mysterious and bizarre he might be, could predict such an outcome.

Or maybe, just maybe, the stranger had somehow known this would happen. Marie nibbled on her lower lip as she considered the possibility.

Perhaps he had led her out here, fully aware of the fact that she would never find her way out, that she would travel in circles forever, that the forest was dark and frightening enough to conjure up many unpleasant images that would drive her slowly insane until death claimed her.

"Stop it, Marie," she whispered. "Stop freaking yourself out."

Climbing to her feet, she reached out for the branch of the tree and hoisted herself up. She winced as her overworked calves protested at being reused so soon. She needed to resume walking. It simply didn't matter how badly she felt all over.

"Well," she said to herself as she brushed some of the caked mud off of her backside, "at least *he* isn't here."

A rumble of thunder crackled overhead, calling attention to the fact that a storm was coming. A warning signal trickled down the length of her spine, inducing her flesh to goose pimple and her nipples to harden.

She knew that eerily familiar danger signal. She'd felt it countless times earlier in the evening. And now, somehow, Marie knew she was not standing in the forest alone anymore. There was another presence here now, a presence that was boring a possessive hole right through her body with his gaze.

"I-I hope the answer is no," she breathed out, "but I'll ask the question anyway."

Her pink tongue darted out to wet her dry lips. She swallowed roughly, fearing that she was about to die, that the mysterious stranger meant to harm her. "Is s-somebody there?"

Chapter 2

He emerged from the shadows. The mysterious stranger. The tall, brooding man with the crystalline eyes. He was dressed in harsh black, from the shoulders of his black greatcoat to the tips of his black boots. His gaze raked the length of her body, hovering overlong at her breasts and then again at the visible slit of material that ran the length of her thigh.

Marie took a reflexive step backward, instinctively drawing the cloak more securely about her. Her breathing hitched as she considered the very real possibility that she was about to die — or be raped — or both...

He was so much larger than she, standing at least six foot three. His musculature was sleek and honed, making her frame appear rather small and inconsequential next to his. And she was tired, so very tired. She could attempt to run, but in the end he'd catch her. "What do you want?" she whispered. "Why are you here?"

One dark eyebrow shot up, delineating a scar on his forehead she hadn't noticed at the exhibit. But then, she'd been too busy staring at his oddly clear, wolverine eyes to notice much else about him. She was noticing the scar now, however. She couldn't help but to wonder how it had gotten there, or more specifically, what woman had put it there. Had she been screaming at the time, clawing at him in a vain attempt to stay alive? Marie took another step backward.

The second eyebrow shot up to join the first. A small smile tugged at the corners of his mouth. "I came to take you home, Marie." He made the assertion quietly, his thick accent definitive. "Now."

Her eyes widened. His gaze tracked the movement, missing nothing, detailing everything. "How do you know my name?" she breathed out.

"I asked around." His large shoulders slightly shrugged, effectively dismissing the subject. Holding out a palm, he directed her to come to him. "I shan't harm you if that's what you're thinking. I'd never harm so lovely a creature."

A creature? My God. He *was* like a wild animal let loose at a formal ceremony—he didn't possess even the smallest amount of social wherewithal.

Affronted by such a backward compliment from such an odd man, she frowned. She considered the fact that now was probably not the time most conducive to debating his good manners or lack thereof, so she decided in the end to overlook it. Knowingly, the corners of his mouth tugged upward again, letting her know he'd gotten the message.

"Look Mister…"

"Sörebo. Fredrik Sörebo."

Marie nodded. She cleared her throat. "Mister Sörebo, I…"

"Please," he interrupted, his gaze drilling into hers, "call me Fredrik," he murmured.

"Fredrik," she repeated, gritting her teeth, "I thank you for offering to help me, but I'm doing just fine on my own. I don't need your assistance."

He chuckled in response, his head slightly shaking. "You have no idea where you are, no clue as to where you are going. This is my land you are lost on, so I cannot, in good conscience, allow such a beautiful woman to roam about unattended." His eyes flicked around the dark forest until they settled once more on her face. "There are wild animals out here, animals large enough to tear you into pieces," he said in low tones.

Marie's large green eyes rounded considerably more as the image he'd just conjured up took firm root in her mind. She drew her hands up and began to rub her arms briskly. "You will take me h-home, then? To the inn I mean?"

"I'll take you home," he quietly promised.

She didn't care for his deliberate exclusion of the last part of her question, but understood at the same time that she had no choice but to go with him, odd or no. She was tired, cold, and the storm was growing closer. She needed to find shelter, even if said shelter was within Fredrik Sörebo's estate. For now she would go. And pray she lived to tell about it.

Squaring her shoulders, Marie nodded toward him. "Very well. I can always call for a taxi from your house, I suppose."

He studied her facial features as he walked the remainder of the space that separated them. A predator's eyes. That's all she saw when she looked at him. "There are no taxis in Göthmoor," he said simply.

A moment later, one muscle-roped arm was flung around her as he drew her in closer to his side. His hand settled possessively on the intimate juncture where her right thigh and hip met. He led her deeper into the woods and down a new path she hadn't seen before. Marie's entire body clenched in nervous reaction. How would she ever get out of this?

The man was strange. And his touch was too familiar.

"Where are we going?" she asked ten minutes later, every bone and muscle in her body screaming in protest. "Are we almost there?" she asked wearily.

"Almost," he confirmed. He squeezed her hip gently, telling her without words that he understood how tired she must be. "I'll bathe you when we reach the castle," he informed her. "It will help your muscles to relax."

Alarmed once again, Marie nibbled at her lower lip. He hadn't said she could take a bath. He had said he would bathe her. There was a difference. A massively big difference.

And then her thoughts were no more when, a few moments later, they rounded a bend and were spit out of the forest and onto a deserted moor. The castle Fredrik had spoken of sat at its tip, as large, dark, and ominous-looking as the man who dwelled within it.

"This is my home," he murmured. "For over three centuries my family has lived within these very walls."

Marie nodded, but said nothing. She wanted to ask him if they had been buried there as well, but decided to hold her tongue. She had a feeling she would need it later. To help her scream.

Her eyes raked over the castle's stone walls. The very tall, very impenetrable-looking stone walls. Swallowing against the lump in her throat, she glanced upward toward Fredrik. The moonlight cast his features in harsh relief, one half of his face left in shadow.

But she could see his eyes. Those damn eyes. And she was starting to understand their promises.

Marie feared that Fredrik would never let her leave this fortress alive.

Chapter 3

Marie stared into the flames crackling before her as her hands nervously rotated the cup of hot tea she'd been given to drink. She knew the hot tea would feel like a soothing balm to her parched throat, but she feared for what it might be laced with.

"Only honey and lemon," Fredrik murmured from the chair across from her, as if reading her thoughts. He smiled that half-smile, amused by her not so subtle hesitation. "I promise." He nodded his head. "Go on and drink it while I draw your bath."

Marie's head shot up. She cleared her throat as she made a valiant effort toward meeting his gaze. "I, uh...I don't want to take a bath." She looked down toward her lap and stared at the teacup in her hands. "I just want to go back to the inn. Please."

Fredrik was quiet for so long that at first Marie thought he hadn't heard her whispered plea. But eventually he spoke, his voice low and controlled. "The storm outside has grown worse, ängel. I think it best that you remain here...with me."

A rumble of thunder loudly boomed as he finished speaking, underscoring the truth to his words. But Marie didn't care. She just wanted to leave.

"I'm tired," she said wearily. "Very tired, very cold, and my body aches." She nervously cleared her throat. "I just want to leave. I don't care how bad it's storming outside. Please. Let me go."

Silence ensued for a drawn-out moment. The only sound that could be heard was that of the flames crackling in the massive fireplace they were seated in front of.

At last Fredrik spoke, breaking the unbearably tense silence. "How old are you?" he asked, ignoring her previous statement.

Marie stared at him. She shook her head slightly, wondering where that question had come from when she'd been speaking of something else entirely. "Twenty-eight. Almost twenty-nine."

"I'm forty-one."

She nodded, then began sipping from her tea. The flavor was good, she quickly decided. If he'd poisoned it, she thought to herself, at least her last sips would be tasty ones. "So I was told."

A dark eyebrow inched up. "Oh? And who told you that?"

"Helena Anders."

"So you've made inquiries about me?" he asked softly.

Marie's cheeks grew hot. She shot her gaze from her host back down to the teacup. "Well," she defensively replied, "you *were* staring at me a great deal. It was only natural to inquire as to who you are."

"Because you're beautiful," he said darkly, his voice a monotone. "The loveliest woman I've ever laid eyes on."

Marie picked at a piece of imaginary lint on her cloak. "There's more to me than that, you know," she said quietly, but bitterly. "A lot more."

And really, was that all men saw when they looked at her? A pleasing face and a plump chest? It was no wonder she shied away from dating, she admitted to herself. No man knew the real Marie and no man cared to get past the physical aspects of her body long enough to understand her. She was just a doll, an ornament, a trophy to put over the fireplace and let her emotionally decay from neglect.

Even her father, as much as she loved him, thought her to be no more than a pretty face.

Then again, who cares, she thought grimly. She was probably about to die or be raped. Worrying about the superficiality of the male species was last on her list of concerns at the moment.

"Then tell me," Fredrik encouraged her as he lifted his own teacup to his lips and took a sip. His gaze found hers and held it. "I want to know everything."

Marie stilled. She wanted to leave, not talk, but she conceded that being polite wouldn't hurt her case. She just hoped this was a good sign, and that the handsomely odd man with the eerie blue eyes didn't make a habit of inquiring into the backgrounds of his victims before he did…things…to them.

"I love to paint," she whispered. "Actually—" she cleared her throat and spoke louder, "I'm quite good at it."

Fredrik inclined his head. "I'm certain you're good at anything you love doing, *ängel*."

Why did he keep calling her that? "I also enjoy writing," she replied, "poetry mostly, but I pen short stories as well." She threw a wayward golden lock over her shoulder as she broke eye contact and stared at her lap. She hated talking about herself with people she knew. Talking about her life with a man who put her on edge made it a thousand times worse. "But those are silly endeavors," she relented, her voice trailing off, "nothing important or meaningful."

"Who told you that?" he asked quietly.

Marie shrugged her shoulders. She set the teacup down and clutched her hands together on her lap as she met his gaze. "Everyone. My father mostly."

"He's wrong. They're all wrong. If you have a gift, never squander it."

She stared at him strangely, wondering why he should care. Finally, she looked away. "I suppose you're right," she whispered.

"I am right."

She shrugged her shoulders but said nothing in reply.

Another interminable silence ensued, the only sound that of the crackling flames, as well as rumbles of thunder and pattering of rain pounding against the castle walls. Marie took a deep breath, wanting to leave, but knowing that even if Fredrik relented and allowed her to go back to the inn—which she doubted he would until he was ready—he'd never take her back during the brunt of such a fierce storm. As solid and impenetrable as the stone walls were, she could still hear the outside elements slashing against them.

Fredrik stood up a moment later, diverting her attention toward him. She looked at him hesitantly, wondering why he was standing.

"I'm going to draw you a hot bath."

Her eyes widened. "But I—"

"—am chilled to the bone and in need of a hot bath."

Marie's teeth sank into her bottom lip as she anxiously studied the man hovering over her. What did he want from her, this reclusive stranger? She'd heard ugly things about him. Terrible things. Unmentionable things. She didn't want to end up like—

"People don't see or understand the real Marie Robb," Fredrik murmured, staring down at her from his powerful six feet and three inches, "because they see only what they want to see, know only what they want to know." He inclined his head before turning from her and walking toward the twisting stairwell. "It's much the same for me."

Marie stared after him, uncertain what she should think. On one hand, she shouldn't have assumed he was a monster just because of village gossip, but on the other hand, kidnapping her was hardly making a strong case for himself. Then again, he hadn't kidnapped her. In fact, she would have been grateful for his assistance was he not so mysteriously peculiar.

And if she still wasn't questioning whether or not he had known her tire would go flat on that deserted back road.

Perhaps he was a monster. But maybe he wasn't. "Fredrik?"

He came to a halt mid-step, then glanced over his shoulder to make eye contact. He raised an eyebrow, but said nothing else.

Marie wrung her hands together in her lap, anxious, nervous, terrified…but wanting to know her fate, needing to know it. She cleared her throat and met his gaze. She didn't care how offended he became by the question she was about to ask. She needed the answer. "Are you going to rape me?" she quietly asked.

He made not a single movement for the longest time. Not a flinch. Not a grimace. Not a nod of the head or a verbal negation. Not anything that would clue her in as to how and what he was feeling and thinking. He was like a statue, Marie thought, as impenetrable and unmoving as the cold stone walls surrounding them. She shivered, wondering if she'd just given him ideas he hadn't contemplated beforehand.

And then at last, after what felt like hours, the corners of his lips tugged upwards into that all-knowing smirk she was now coming to associate as belonging to Fredrik Sörebo. "No." He turned away from her and strode up the remainder of the spiraling staircase at a leisurely gait. "I won't need to rape you, *ängel*."

Chapter 4

Marie sat in the intricately carved bathtub, the hot water lulling the aches in her muscles and bones. The water level reached to her waist, exposing her breasts to the chill in the air outside of the gold-gilded basin. Her nipples were hard and elongated, dark beige with a sprinkling of dusky rose at the tips.

She glanced around the bathroom, trying to locate some sort of washcloth she could use to scrub her body with. She'd relented and decided to take the bath she didn't want to take because she hadn't known what else to do. Might as well make the most of it, she thought on a sigh.

A pad of sweet smelling soap sat to her left, but no washing towel was anywhere within the vicinity. As she looked around, it dawned on her that there were no towels at all laying about, nothing even to dry herself off with when she finished bathing. Apparently her host had forgotten to leave her a couple of them before he'd left her to her bath—she hoped.

Her host. Marie sighed, thinking back to those words he had spoken to her from the staircase. "*I won't need to rape you*, ängel," he had said.

She stilled as she considered what he could have possibly meant by that bold statement. At the exhibit, she reluctantly admitted, her body had responded to his stare in ways it shouldn't have. But that had been upon first glance. Before she'd known who he was, before she'd heard the village gossip, and before he'd scared her half to death with his odd proclamation that she would belong to him.

Belong to him how? Like an exotic pet he kept and never let go?

Mentally and physically exhausted, she took a deep breath and twisted her hair into a quasi-bun on top of her head. That accomplished, she laid back, lowered herself into the water, and closed her eyes. Her nipples poked up through the liquid, not enough in the tub to conceal them.

"This has been such a long day," she said tiredly, her voice scratchy from exhaustion. "Such a very long day."

Sighing, she allowed her body to be soothed by the steaming water. She wanted to think of nothing, consider nothing. Later she could deal with her predicament. Later she could contemplate her body's prior reaction to the reclusive Mr. Sörebo. Later she could figure out what to do. For now, she just wanted to relax. It was the last thought she entertained as she drifted off into a deep slumber.

Unknown minutes later, Marie slowly emerged from the mindless fog of sleep as tendrils of desire began coiling in her belly. She was so out of it that she couldn't register why her body was turned on to a fever-pitch, only that it was. She was so near to climax, so deliciously close. She smiled, her slumbering brain idly wondering if she was experiencing her first ever wet dream.

It felt as though a naked body was holding hers, cradling her wet flesh from behind. Fingers—oh God the most exquisitely callused fingers—were penetrating her vagina as a thumb briskly rubbed her clit in methodic circles. "Mmmm," she murmured, her eyes still closed, "yes."

More fingers. She opened her thighs for them, wanting them there. They filled her flesh, massaging her clit. So good. So incredibly good. On a moan, she opened her legs even wider, needing completion.

A hand at her breast. Fingers plucking her nipples. Fingers thrusting deeply inside of her. She wanted this. Needed this. It felt so—"*Oh God.*"

Marie's eyes flew open as an orgasm ripped through her insides, causing her belly to contract and her nipples to lengthen impossibly further. She groaned, releasing her juices all over the fingers, wanting more.

She had barely come down enough from nirvana to register the fact that the fingers were real before she was being turned around and a long, thick cock was poised at her entrance, preparing to impale her. Wide emerald eyes met possessive sapphire ones.

"Fredrik," she breathed out.

He searched her gaze for a long moment, giving her the time to tell him no, giving her a chance to dismiss him. She hesitated, her body and mind pulling her in two opposite directions.

Her mind told her to be frightened, to climb off of him and run. But her body...

She wet her lips. She was so turned on. So totally aroused—

He surged upwards, filling her completely. She gasped.

"Mmmm...*ängel*," he murmured, his teeth gritting at the feel of her flesh enveloping his. He sucked in his breath. "Your pussy feels so good," he said hoarsely. "*Så trång och skön*—So tight and good."

Straddling his lap, Marie blew out a breath, her arousal playing tug-of-war with her brain. He was incredible to look at. Not beautiful perhaps, but harsh and masculine. Primal.

His chest—so powerful, sprinkled with black hair that tapered off into a vee at the place where they joined. His cock—so thick and filling, pulsing even now inside of her.

And his eyes…those hypnotic icy blue orbs that held so many secrets. What did they see when they looked at her?

"Fredrik," she whispered, "I…" *Don't want to end up like her.*

"Shh. Do not fight this."

"Please," she begged, "this…" *Is frightening. My God, what if the things I was told are true?*

"Marie, *ängel*," he murmured, "do not fight this."

Again, she hesitated. She was too aroused to think clearly, she decided, blowing out a breath and blinking. Her fingernails dug into his shoulders.

He slammed his shaft upward, filling her entirely, making her gasp, as he simultaneously covered her lips with his own. Thrusting his tongue into her mouth, his fingers dug into the flesh of her hips as he guided her body up and down the length of him. He broke the kiss as he sucked in his breath. "Yes, Marie. *God, yes*," he ground out.

Marie's breathing grew labored. She shouldn't want to finish this, shouldn't crave to finish this. But she did. It made no sense. It defied the logic of the situation. If any logic even existed.

Maybe she was still dreaming. Maybe it was just a dream…

And then he was popping one of her nipples into his mouth and sucking on it from base to tip, his eyes closed, his breathing heavy, like it was the most delicious thing he'd ever tasted. She quit fighting the arousal altogether, allowing herself to feel, to enjoy. Groaning, she sat up on her knees, then thrust downwards, re-impaling herself on his cock.

He groaned in reaction, releasing her nipple long enough to further encourage her. "Yes, *ängel*," he said thickly. "Move up and down on me…just like that."

She rode him hard, up and down, over and over, again and again. Her breasts jiggled with every movement, tempting him to palm her full flesh in each hand, stroking the nipples, plucking at them, making her convulse from the pleasure of it. She was so turned on. So incredibly aroused…

And then she was coming, screaming from the intensity of it. Her vagina began to contract, pulsing around his shaft, milking him for release. "*Oh God. Oh yes. Oh God!*"

"*Jag behöver dig,*" he groaned. Grabbing her by the hips, he thrust upwards once, twice, three times more, and then he burst. Closing his eyes, his muscles corded and tensed. His nostrils flared as he buried his face in her neck and spurted himself deep within her.

"I need you," he murmured against the flesh of her neck. "God, how I need you."

* * * * *

Fredrik held Marie tightly against him in the tepid waters, her back to his chest. Stroking her hair, he allowed her to sleep in his arms, warm, wet flesh cradled by warm, wet flesh.

Kissing her temple, he sighed deeply.

So many thoughts intruded. So many memories.

But Marie…this woman was different. Not like the others. Especially not like Helena Anders' daughter.

Twisting a lock of Marie's golden hair around his finger, Fredrik murmured her name, then kissed her temple again.

He could not let her go.

Amazing, really, but from the first moment he'd spotted her ambling around Göthmoor two days past he had known she was the one.

He would not let her go.

She was different...so unusual and intoxicatingly naïve. She would never turn on him once she was bound to him.

He needed her.

He'd been dead inside for so long. No joys. No sorrows. No dreams. No nightmares. No nothing. Just a void...a black abyss.

Fredrik rolled one of Marie's nipples between his thumb and forefinger as he considered the sleeping woman in his arms.

Long hair the color of flowing honey. Wide, innocent, luminous eyes. And so trusting...naïve to the point of being a danger to herself.

Kissing her temple one last time, Fredrik continued to tweak at her nipple as his other hand reached down to stroke her clit. His erection prodded at her entrance from behind.

"Wake up, *ängel*," he murmured in her ear. "It's time to bind you to me."

Chapter 5

Fredrik carried a groggy Marie from the bathing chamber into his bedroom through a wide corridor that joined the two spaces. Candles lit in wall sconces flicked about the room, providing a dull glow.

Sitting her on the edge of the bed, he undid the topknot she had wound her hair into and let it flow all about her. "So beautiful," he said possessively, his eyes traveling the length of her. "So very beautiful."

Reaching for and grabbing the flesh of a thigh in either hand, he slowly opened her legs until her glistening labia was on prominent display. His murmured words of appreciation caused her body to respond and desire to knot in her belly.

Marie sucked in her breath as she shoved at his hands in a vain attempt to thwart him. "Fredrik," she said smokily, her voice husky from sleep and arousal, "this is not a good idea. In fact, it's a very bad one."

"You want me. I want you." He rubbed her clit in slow circles with the pad of his thumb, his erection growing as he felt her tremble for him. "And I'm not letting you go."

Final. Definitive.

"But Fredrik—oomph!"

Marie's eyes widened as she was flung backwards onto the bed. Her buttocks were still at the edge, her thighs spread wide, her clit and labia on display. The black silk sheets beneath her felt cool and inviting, a contrast against her fevered flesh. "Fredrik, I—*oh*."

His mouth came down then, covering her entire center. On his knees before her at the edge of the bed, he gripped both thighs and pressed them apart as far as they would comfortably budge.

Apparently he was done with words, done with trying to coax her into submission verbally. Instead he would do it with sensation…with tongue and lips, sucking and slurping sounds, guttural sounds of pleasure erupting from the back of his throat as he drank of her.

"*Oh God.*" His tongue curled around her clit, causing Marie to throw her head back on a moan. "Yes…*please.*"

Bringing the bud between his teeth, he went in for the kill, sucking vigorously on her clit, wanting her to climax violently for him — because of him.

The pleasure she felt was so powerful it was painful. Knots of arousal twined in her belly, clutching her womb.

And then he stopped.

Marie's eyes flicked open and widened. She took a deep breath and looked down at him from between her legs.

Raising his head slowly from between her thighs, Fredrik sought out her gaze and held it. His breathing was harsh, his control hanging on by a thread. Light from a waning candle flicked once across his face, illuminating the ice of his eyes, before snuffing out completely.

"Yes or no?" he asked, his nostrils flaring. "Do you want me? Despite…everything." He reached out and ran a thumb over one of her hardened nipples. "Yes or no?" he murmured.

Marie panted for breath, her entire body on fire. He had been right all along, of course. He wouldn't have to rape her to take her. She'd give him her body willingly and they both knew it. This was just his arrogant way of making the distinction clear.

Rather than answering him with words, Marie draped her thighs around his neck, twined a foot around the back of his head, and lowered his face back down to her labia. She moaned when his lips and tongue found her clit once more, working her back up toward a fevered pitch in scarce moments. "*Oh yes.*"

Fredrik groaned, his erection hard as steel against his stomach. He suckled from her clit in hard movements, not stopping, never relenting, keeping the pressure firm and torturously pleasurable, even as her hips began to rear up and her moaning intensified. "Mmmm," he drawled against her flesh, vibrating its center, "*mmmmmm.*"

"*Fredrik.*"

She shouldn't want him, shouldn't crave him. She shouldn't desire the touch of such a strange, reclusive man.

"*Fredrik.*" Twining her thighs around his neck, she lurched her hips upward, pressing her clit into his mouth as though she wanted him to devour it.

And then she was coming. Hard. Violent. The waves of pleasure overtook her, inducing her to throw back her head and scream. Blood rushed toward her face, heating it. Tremors went off throughout her body, elongating her nipples to the point of broaching pain. "*Oh God.*"

She had no time to contemplate the insanity of the situation, no time to second-guess the invitation of her body that she'd offered to the mysterious Fredrik Sörebo. His body was covering hers within seconds, his thick erection pressing into her, filling her wet flesh completely.

Rolling both of them toward the middle of the bed, he never allowed their bodies to disjoin. Coming back down on top of her to cover her body with his own, he wound his arms around the back of her neck, through her hair, grasping onto it as though he owned her.

Marie shuddered out a breath, moistening her lips as she regarded him. Raising her hips, she tangled her legs around his waist and held on for a hard ride. She was done with worrying, done with holding a part of herself back.

At least for tonight. For this one night she would think of nothing but pleasure, of giving herself to this man.

"Yes, *ängel*," he gritted out as he rammed his cock into her, reaching the mouth of her womb. "*Knulla mig*. Fuck me."

The icy fire of his eyes coupled with his thickly whispered words of desire sent another tendril of arousal coursing through her body. She clutched at him with her legs, inviting him to explore her. "I want you Fredrik," she admitted, not caring about whether or not she would regret saying those words to him come morning, "take all of me. Now."

Twining a thick golden tress securely about his hand, he held onto her like a possession he would never let go of, groaning as he sank into her pussy over and over again. "*Ja*, baby." *Yes, baby.*

She shifted her hips upward, meeting his thrusts as they were given to her. Her nails raked down the steel of his back, a single red droplet of blood marring the pristine whiteness of her manicure. "Harder," she moaned, grinding into him as he quickened the pace of his thrusting, "Fuck me harder."

"As you wish, *ängel*," he ground out.

Beads of sweat broke out on his forehead as Fredrik rewarded her enthusiasm for his lovemaking by giving her what she'd asked for. His strokes became faster and deeper as he used his free hand to nudge her legs from around his middle. Never letting go of her hair, he used his other hand to throw one of her legs over his shoulder, putting her flesh at an angle conducive to the deepest of penetrations. "Is this what you want?" he asked hoarsely.

Marie moaned long and needfully, her head thrown back, her neck bared to him like an offering, as his cock slammed into her again and again. The sounds of their flesh slapping into and against each other heightened their mutual arousal.

"I asked you if this is what you want," Fredrik said demandingly, his jaws clenched.

"*Yes*," she groaned.

"How does my cock feel inside of you?" he gritted out, his muscles corded, as he pummeled into her mercilessly. When her only answer was a whimper, he slammed harder and asked her again. "How does my cock feel inside of you?"

"*Good*," she groaned. "*Oh God...so good.*"

He rewarded her answer by plunging further, penetrating her as deeply as possible. He slammed into her for endless minutes, each thrust bringing her closer to completion.

And then she was contracting around him, her flesh milking his as her tremors began and she gave herself up to another violent climax in his arms. "*Fredrik...oh God, Fredrik.*"

"Yes, *ängel*," he shouted out hoarsely, his own orgasm overpowering him, "*yes.*"

They came together, their peak harsh and unrelenting. Neither of them had ever experienced pleasure like this with another. Not once. Not ever. And they both knew it.

Minutes later, they drifted off to sleep in each other's embrace. The last coherent thought Marie entertained that night revolved around a vague flickering of awareness that her hair was still wound around Fredrik's hand.

He wanted to keep her, she thought. Maybe forever.

And then unconsciousness overtook her and she knew no more.

Chapter 6

"What are you saying to me?" Marie's eyes widened as she whispered the question to the older woman.

"I'm saying he's a monster," Helena Anders tonelessly replied, her lifeless obsidian eyes looking at Marie but not seeing her.

Marie reached out and took the older woman's hand in her own. She glanced over her shoulder to make certain the stranger wasn't watching them before she turned back to Helena. "What did he do?" she breathed out.

No response.

She glanced back over her shoulder, her heartbeat picking up. He would return any moment. His attention would be diverted from her for only a minute or so longer. She needed to know what had become of...

"Sophie was a good girl," Helena said in hushed tones.

Marie whipped her head back around to regard her. The woman's eyes were like black glass. Shark's eyes. Doll's eyes. So dead and lifeless. Her lips were puckered, bloodless. Her hair straight and black as sackcloth. Her skin a pasty white.

"She didn't deserve it," Helena droned on.

"Didn't deserve what?"

Silence.

Marie gritted her teeth. Time was running out. He would come back. She didn't want him to know they'd been speaking of him. He would come back. And he would know. Somehow he would know...

Marie's head tossed back and forth on the black silk pillow. Beads of perspiration formed on her brow. "Tell me," she muttered in her sleep. "Tell me what he did."

"He killed her." Helena's parched lips turned upward, forming a cruel slash of a smile. "Raped her and murdered her. Cut her into pieces and threw her to the dogs."

"Oh my God." Marie's hand left the old woman's and pressed against her mouth. Her stomach felt queasy, her knees too weak to stand. "I'm so sorry, Helena," she whispered, "so very sorry."

"She was a good girl," Helena repeated as if she hadn't heard her. "Sophie was a good girl."

Marie was about to respond when the old woman's eyes lit up and bore into hers, the first sign Marie had seen all evening that intelligence and comprehension lurked somewhere in the back of Helena Anders' mind. "He'll do the same to you," she stated tonelessly, as if they were discussing what they'd had for breakfast. "If you allow him near you, the same will become of you."

Marie glanced back over her shoulder. She didn't see him yet, but she knew he was coming. She could sense it, feel him drawing closer. She turned back toward the old woman to tell her never to repeat what they had spoken of.

"She was a good girl," Helena said, her eyes losing their luster once more. Black ice. They looked so much like black ice.

Marie swallowed, bile rising in her throat. "Yes," she murmured, "poor..."

"...Sophie," Marie mumbled in her sleep, perspiration forming between her breasts. "Poor Sophie."

* * * * *

A candle was snuffed out from across the room, a pair of icy blue eyes watching everything.

Fredrik strode the length of the room and resumed his place in the bed next to Marie. Wiping the droplets of sweat from her face and breasts, he cradled her into his arms and held tightly.

For ten years he had existed alone in a void, no light to penetrate the darkness. He had sought out paid companionship when his physical needs had become great, but had otherwise remained alone.

Perhaps...perhaps he had become that very thing Helena said he was. Maybe he was a monster.

Fredrik tightened his hold on Marie, craning his neck to place a soft kiss atop her head. "I'm sorry, *ängel*," he murmured against her temple, "but I won't let you leave me. Not even for a moment."

Chapter 7

"Where are my clothes?"

Marie clutched the black silk sheet to her breasts, protecting herself from Fredrik's gaze. She worried her lip as she watched him watch her, wondering what was going through his mind, wondering what he would do or say.

What she had done last night was wrong. Incredibly, stupidly, wrong. Her father, she thought perversely, probably wouldn't be surprised if he found out she was in such a tenuous position…he'd just consider it further proof that she was an idiot, a thoughtless doll in need of a man to take care of her.

Of course, she reminded herself, her father would probably never find out what had become of her. No one would for that matter. The only people that might realize she was absent were the inn owners, and even they would probably just chalk her disappearance up to another flighty American deciding to leave and venture onward to bluer skies.

She had to face the reality of the situation. She was as good as dead if she didn't find a way to escape the man with the haunted eyes. But she *would* find a way to leave him.

Her father might believe her to be a shrinking violet, but Marie knew better. Deep down inside was a fighter, a fighter that was tired of being walked on. She'd show them all, she vowed to herself. She would make it out of here alive and she would show them all.

"I burned them."

Marie's eyes widened in shock. She had not been expecting to hear that. She was surprised into speechlessness for a tense moment. "You *burned* my clothes?" she breathed out, not believing she'd heard him correctly.

"Yes," Fredrik repeated, walking toward where she sat on the bed, "I burned them."

She blinked a few times in rapid succession as she considered what this did to her escape plans. Running around naked in the pitch dark woods had definitely not been a part of them. Could this damn man foretell all of her plans without her even uttering them?

"I don't believe this," Marie stated incredulously, her voice rising in decibel with her anger. "Why in the hell would you burn my clothes?"

Fredrik sat on the edge of the bed and lifted a sardonic eyebrow. "So you can't leave me," he said simply.

Good God. The man really could predict the future. Marie didn't know whether to laugh or cry. Instead, she clutched the silk sheet tighter with one hand while using the other to wave toward her captor. "What exactly am I supposed to wear?"

The other eyebrow came up to meet the first. "Nothing, *ängel*," he softly replied.

Marie's body had an immediate reaction to what he'd said and the way he'd said it. She squelched the traitorous feeling, knowing it was precisely that reaction that had gotten her into this mess to begin with. There would be no repeat performances of last night.

Her nostrils flared. "I demand to be given some clothes," she gritted out.

"No."

"No?" she shrieked. "No?!" Marie's lips attempted to form words, but no sounds came out.

Fredrik took advantage of the moment, pulling the sheet away from her while she was still too shocked to retaliate. The expensive bolt of black silk fell to the floor, discarded and forgotten. "That is correct, *ängel*. No."

Scooting closer to her on the bed, he reached out and lifted one of her breasts into the palm of his hand. His thumb swept over the nipple, causing Marie to suck in her breath.

"Fredrik," she breathed out, "I don't want—"

"One week," he said quietly, steely control threaded through his voice. "I ask for only one week of your time." His gaze met hers. "If after a week you still wish to leave me, you will be free to depart this place."

Marie closed her eyes briefly, the image such an arrangement conjured up in her mind a confusing one. Instead of imagining violence and death as she rightly should have, she saw only pleasure and hedonism. Fredrik's body, his touch, his kisses…his lovemaking.

She opened her eyes and met his gaze. "Why?" she whispered. "Why do you want me to stay for a week and then let me leave?"

"I don't want you to leave, Marie. You misunderstand me. I said I want you to stay and that when one week has gone by I will give you the option of departing."

Alive?

No. No. If he'd meant to kill her, wouldn't he have done so by now? Maybe. But then again…maybe not. Perhaps he liked to toy with his victims, give them hope, make them think they stood a chance of escape. Or perhaps he'd meant specifically what he'd said, no symbolic meaning intended.

"And what will happen during this week?" Marie asked, hesitantly curious.

Fredrik was quiet for a long moment. He let go of her breast and broke eye contact. Sighing deeply, his eyes flicked about the massive bedroom.

"I will get to know the real Marie Robb," he at last stated. "And you will get to know the real Fredrik Sörebo."

Marie took a deep breath and exhaled slowly as she absently glanced toward the ceiling. "And the clothes?" she inquired in a monotone, not seeing how she really had a choice but to give him his week.

"No clothes," Fredrik answered, his eyes flicking over her body as he spoke. "I want you naked for the entire week."

Part II:
The Seduction

Chapter 8

The chill in the air hardened Marie's nipples into tight points. Naked, she shivered as she ambled through the estate gardens with a fully clothed Fredrik, her hand in his.

The sun was looming straight overhead, so it wasn't terribly cold outside, yet the shivers continued regardless. She wasn't certain if it was the weather or the man beside her causing the reaction, but she had her guesses.

Uncharacteristic though it was, Marie had decided to let herself go for this week. There was no point in doing anything less, and really, she didn't want to. So a week it was. A week of Fredrik. A week of sex. A week of no clothing.

She felt erotic, immensely turned on, though he hadn't so much as intimately touched her yet. There was something deliciously wicked and provocative about being totally divested of clothing while outdoors, not to mention while in the presence of a powerful man fully clothed.

She'd been turned on all day long. She would have made love with him if he'd asked and yet he'd made no move to cover her body with his. But she knew he would...eventually. And the not knowing when, the not knowing where...that was as much an aphrodisiac as her lack of attire. She wondered if Fredrik realized that, and guessed that he probably had.

Fredrik. The man was an enigma. Strange and mysterious, so many secrets, so reclusive and isolated. Marie could only wonder at which of the stories she'd heard of him were true.

Though one thing was certain. The more time she spent at his side watching him gaze about his garden of all things—such tenderness in his expression, such peace—well, it became more and more difficult to accept Helena Anders' version of events as the gospel truth.

What had really happened that night ten years past? she wondered to herself for the thousandth time. Was this man at her side truly capable of such...atrocity? Could he rape a young woman? Then cut her flesh up into pieces and feed it to wild animals to hide the evidence of his crime?

Perhaps "could he" wasn't the best question to ask, Marie considered with a shiver. Perhaps "would he" was more apropos. Certainly he harbored the necessary physical strength to commit so heinous an act...but *would* he? That was the true question.

"You are quiet, *ängel*," Fredrik stated, breaking the silence between them. "I was telling you that this would be a lovely place to either paint or set up a desk and write." He smiled. "I'm rambling on and you've heard not a word of it."

"Sorry." Marie cleared her throat as she glanced around the gardens. "I'm listening now. You've got my full attention."

Truly, it was an extraordinarily beautiful place. So many colors, so much life. Beautiful, exotic plants and flowers, lush green trees manicured to perfection.

Such a light contrast to the dark man who tended to them.

"Right here," Fredrik said, motioning with his hand toward an elegant chair that looked right at home within the massive garden structure. "This is where I typically sit and have coffee every morning. It would be a lovely place to paint."

But Marie was paying no attention to the chair amidst the gardens. She was gawking instead at the easel and paints that had already been set up beside it. Her eyes shot up to meet Fredrik's. "You paint, too?"

"Sometimes." He shrugged dismissively. "But I'm not very good at it." He nodded toward the easel. "I suspect you'll be much better at it. Go on. Try it out."

Marie blinked, her expression hesitant, wondering if this was some sort of weird trick. Here she stood, after all, naked as the day she was born, completely exposed to the man at her side, and he wanted her to...paint. She wasn't used to men taking an interest in anything about her besides her outward appearance and didn't know what to make of this.

She'd hand it to Fredrik for one thing—

He'd managed to shock her.

"Okay," she finally said, frowning. She still couldn't help but to feel this was somehow a trick, but then that made no sense really. She sighed, deciding it wasn't worth thinking about. "If you insist, then I would be more than happy to paint for a while."

Fredrik motioned toward the easel as he seated himself in the chair across from her standing position. A coffeepot and two coffee cups had been set on a small table next to him. Marie had no idea how they had gotten there and she was too focused on her thoughts to think much about it. This man, this oddly mysterious man, wanted her to...paint.

Shrugging her shoulders, she picked up a brush and did just that. And what's more, it felt great. She loved this freedom of expression, this outlet for her emotions, and she always had. Ever since she'd been a little girl she'd had the ability to lose herself in the world of art, painting away the ugly parts of life and replacing them with the beautiful.

When she painted, she felt...alive. So incredibly energized and full of passion. And it showed. She was too absorbed in her work to realize it, but the man sitting across from her could see the vitality in her movements, could feel it in the very air about them.

Two hours had gone by when at last she'd finished. Marie had set out to recreate Fredrik amongst his gardens and she'd done just that. In painstaking detail. It dawned on her only after the fact that she'd forgotten to include the scar on his forehead, that ugly reminder of the things she'd been told about him.

Had she unconsciously omitted it on purpose? And if she had, was it because she didn't want to believe what she'd heard, regardless to whether or not it was the truth? Or was it possible she was beginning not to believe those evil things about him at all?

"It's wonderful, *ängel*," Fredrik murmured from behind her. Sliding his callused hands around to the front of her, he palmed her breasts, rolling the nipples between thumbs and forefingers, and studied the portrait.

Startled, Marie jumped a bit in reaction, not having realized he had moved to stand behind her until she'd felt his hands massaging her breasts. She closed her eyes and took a deep breath, immediately aroused. "Thank you."

"You're welcome," he said in low tones, plucking at the tight points, making them lengthen further. "In fact, very welcome. You recreated the gardens to perfection. It's breathtaking."

"So are you," she whispered.

Fredrik's hands stilled. He grew quiet, giving Marie time to regret what she'd just admitted aloud.

And yet...she didn't. She didn't regret saying it at all.

She sighed, wondering what in the hell was wrong with her.

Fredrik's fingers resumed their lazy exploration of her nipples. "No need to tell me lies, *ängel*. We agreed on a week. Words won't change that." His voice was harsh, stark. Like he had expected more from her than falsehoods and was disappointed when he'd been given them.

Only she wasn't lying. He *was* breathtaking to her. Physically, she reminded herself. Physically, he was breathtaking. She refused to think beyond the physical, didn't want to let a man get behind the emotional barricades that had taken a lifetime to erect.

Especially not him.

But Marie's reasons for not wanting him under her skin no longer solely revolved around the mysterious death of Sophie Anders. They also revolved around the fact that this man was able to see into her soul without being invited in, he was able to second-guess her motivations, comprehend what made her tick. That reality frightened her as much as any malicious gossip. Perhaps even more so.

Fredrik Sörebo wasn't the only person standing in the garden with stone walls erected around their emotions. And, Marie thought somewhat sadly, he wasn't the only one that thought himself unworthy, and for that reason incapable of letting those walls fall to the ground. In that moment, she felt more connected to him than she wished she did.

Shrugging his hands from off of her breasts, she slowly turned around to confront him. "I didn't lie." Meeting his gaze, she allowed him in just far enough to see that she was telling the truth as she saw it. Perhaps other women didn't find him visually appealing—she didn't know. But she did. And that's all that mattered. "I didn't lie," she whispered, her eyelids shuttering.

"Marie—"

She quickly placed a palm over his mouth then closed her eyes altogether. The stark hopelessness she saw in his icy blue gaze was very real—and she didn't want to be moved by it. And yet...

Her eyes opened. "I didn't lie." Taking his hand, she led him back toward the chair he'd been occupying while she had painted. Nudging him toward it, she went down to her knees in front of him after he'd sat and slowly unzipped his pants.

Fredrik sucked in his breath. The erection he'd sustained all afternoon long became impossibly harder, so torturous it was painful. The feel of Marie's hands wrapped around his flesh coupled with the knowledge that she had come to him without coaxing was enough to make him shiver. "What are you doing to me, beautiful *ángel*?" he said hoarsely. "My God, what are you doing to me?"

He hadn't meant literally, of course, and they both knew it.

Marie's green eyes clashed with Fredrik's pained blue ones. He needed her right now. Whatever had happened ten years ago had affected this man as greatly as it had affected Helena Anders. When she gazed into his eyes, she didn't see a monster. She saw just a man. An ordinary, vulnerable man.

He needed her. And strange as it was, she needed him too. She simply didn't care about anything else right now.

"Fredrik?"

"Yes?" he asked quietly.

"You are worthy."

His fathomless eyes widened a bit, surprised and moved as he was by her heartfelt proclamation. And then he thought of nothing else as Marie's lips found his manhood, her tongue coiling around its head, reeling his erection into the warmth of her mouth. "*Christ.*"

Marie took him all of the way in, from crown to root, sucking up and down the length of him, again and again. She felt his muscles bunch and tense from the pleasure as his steel-hard cock disappeared into the depths of her throat. "Mmmm," she purred in the back of her throat, feeling his pleasure as though it were her own. "Mmmmm."

"*Christ — Marie.*" Fredrik's breathing grew heavy as he watched her full lips devour him. Sucking sounds rose up, mingling with and overpowering the faint sound of birds chirping in the gardens.

He reached out for her face, brushing her long honey-colored hair over her shoulder, wanting to watch her love him with her mouth. Her eyes were closed, her breathing dense, the expression on her face one of carnal rapture. It was enough to shatter any remnants of control he'd once held onto.

"Yes, *ängel*," he ground out, "your mouth feels so good on me."

And then he was gritting his teeth and closing his eyes as she sped up the pace of her sucking, smacking sounds from flesh meeting saliva growing prominent.

He had thought to make love to her, to empty himself deep inside of her womb, but she wasn't stopping, wasn't relenting, wasn't letting go. Up and down her mouth went, faster and faster, latched onto him as though it belonged there. "*Christ.*"

On a groan of ecstasy, Fredrik's entire body shuddered and convulsed as he ejaculated into her mouth and throat. The pleasure was so intense it bordered on the painful.

Emotions of the heart mingled with sexual hedonism of the body. Lust coupled with affection.

He wasn't given time to come down from one high before Marie sent him climbing toward another. Fingers opened up the buttons on his shirt and ran through the crisp hair on his chest, over his nipples. Her mouth enveloped the flesh of his scrotum, sucking leisurely on him. "Jesus," he groaned.

Marie sat before him, naked and vulnerable, yet feeling very powerful. His cock was growing thick and erect...because of her. His breathing was rapid and raspy...because of her. Perhaps he even felt worthy...and perhaps it was because of her.

The wetness between her legs intensified as she once again wrapped her lips and tongue around his manhood. His moans of pleasure further aroused her, causing her to suck faster and harder, wanting to hear him moan louder, needing to feel the proof of his desire for her.

She sat on her knees between his legs and sucked on him, getting lost in the sounds of his guttural groans, growing moist from his obvious pleasure. She continued to suck for at least ten minutes more, ten long pleasurable minutes, until he was once again close to bursting and her jaw had gone numb from maintaining the same openmouthed position for so long.

"Marie," he panted, his breathing harsh. "Climb onto my lap, *ängel*. Come sit on my lap."

She did as she'd been bidden, rising up from her knees to straddle her legs around Fredrik's hips. Clutching at either side of his face, she covered his mouth with her own as she sank down onto his erection and seated him fully within her.

"Oh God," she gasped, breaking the kiss as she began to ride him, "you feel so good, Fredrik. Your cock feels so good."

"So does your tight pussy, *ängel*." He grabbed her hips and slammed her down on top of him with deep, fast thrusts. "I want this pussy forever, Marie," he said with a clenched jaw. "When I wake up in the morning, I want to feel it fucking me. When I take lunch in the afternoons, I want it for dessert. When I get hungry at night, I want it at my beck and call, always ready to pleasure me."

Marie groaned as she threw her head back, baring her throat to him, riding him fast, wanting him to be a part of her. He bit down on her neck, holding her there, his fingers digging into the flesh of her hips.

And then she was coming, groaning, the intensity of her orgasm overpowering her. Her flesh contracted around his, coaxing out his own release, causing him to erupt within her. "*Fredrik*."

Clutching her hips tightly, he met her flesh with thrusts of his own, ramming into her as his cock spurted. With a shout of completion, he emptied himself into her body, shuddering from the intensity of it.

And when they came down, their bodies still joined together, they held each other without speaking, cuddled together in mutual exhaustion. They stayed like that, clutching one another as the sun sank below the horizon, illuminating the gardens with shades of vibrant color.

Chapter 9

"Checkmate."

"Damn."

Marie smiled as she glanced up from the chessboard toward Fredrik's disgruntled expression. "Oh come on, you won one time out of three." She batted her eyelashes teasingly. "One out of three isn't so bad."

He mumbled something under his breath, but winked at her good-naturedly. "The thing about beautiful angels, I'm discovering, is that when it comes to winning, they are vicious devils."

Marie smiled, but said nothing.

Silence ensued, the only sound that of the flames crackling in the gaming parlor's fireplace…a sound Marie was quickly growing accustomed to. There were no televisions in this old stone fortress, no modern appliances, not even a single clock so far as she could tell. It was easy to lose oneself in the past here, to forget they were living in the twenty-first century, rather than in a time far removed.

"What are you thinking?" Fredrik asked quietly from the chair across from hers. He picked up his glass of wine and sipped from it. "You've grown quiet."

"I was just thinking how much of a relic this old place is," she admitted on a shrug. "Not that it isn't beautiful because it's the most wonderfully unique home I've ever seen. But why is it you never had the castle modernized?"

His gaze bore right into her, never blinking. "Because when you try to change something that's perfect already the result always becomes rather ugly."

Marie nibbled on her lower lip as she studied him. He was speaking in double entendres, she knew, but wasn't quite certain if she understood exactly what he'd meant by it.

"Are you cold, *ängel*?" Fredrik asked, setting his glass of wine back down on the tabletop beside him. "I can throw another log onto the fire if that's the case."

"No." Marie shook her head slightly. "I'm quite warm, thank you."

"Then why are your nipples so hard?" he said thickly.

Marie's head shot up. She glanced toward Fredrik's lap and instantly noticed he had a large and impressive arousal bulging inside of his pants. The lids of his eyes were heavy, his gaze glazed over with desire.

She grew immediately wet in reaction, her nipples hardening even further.

"What's this?" she asked playfully, her own voice lower in tone than normal. "You don't want to play another game of chess?"

He ignored her teasing banter and held out a hand to her. "Come to me, Marie."

It didn't take an Einstein to figure out why Fredrik wanted her there, nor did one need a high IQ to realize that she desired to give him what he craved. Every moment that they spent in each other's company strengthened the mutual bond they shared that was at once emotional and fundamentally sexual.

Never, not once, had Marie dared give her heart to a man. And now she feared that the very thing she'd so long dreaded was coming to pass against her will. She was becoming vulnerable to Fredrik Sörebo, to a man many called a monster.

"All right," she replied as she stood, "I'm coming."

When she reached his side, she dropped to her knees before him and settled her naked body between his legs. Unzipping his slacks, she freed his erection and swirled her tongue around the pre-ejaculate covered tip until she felt him tense beneath her.

"This is what you want, isn't it Fredrik?" She licked at him again, toying with him a bit. "You like it when I suck you off, don't you?" she whispered seductively.

"I don't like it," he amended, "I love it." His callused fingers ran through her hair, brushing it back. "Same as I love your willingness and desire to please me," he murmured. "At least like this."

She smiled, running the steel velvet tip across her cheek, brushing it across her lips. "Do you really want me to stay here forever, Fredrik?"

"Forever and a day," he countered softly, meaningfully. "Forever and a day."

Marie closed her eyes, lowered her mouth onto his shaft, and sucked him off until he fell asleep in the chair, replete and content.

* * * * *

"What are you looking at?"

Surprised he'd woken back up, Marie gestured toward the album of photographs sitting in Fredrik's lap to emphasize her meaning as she sat down on the arm of the chair he was seated in. She'd only been gone long enough to get a drink. His pants were still unzipped from when she'd had him in her mouth a few hours ago, the black hair on his hard belly disappearing into a thin line out of sight inside of the expensive material.

His clear blue eyes flicked over her nude body and hovered at her breasts, inducing her nipples to harden.

"Pictures, *ängel*."

She rolled her eyes and grinned. "I figured out that much, Fredrik." She threw a hand toward the photographs in question. "But what, or who rather, are they of?"

He shrugged. "A little of everybody. My parents before they died, my older brother before he died, and me..." He glanced away and cleared his throat.

...before I died.

The thought hovered there between them, those unspoken words. Marie instinctively knew that he would have said them aloud had he not thought better of it first.

She decided against pressing him for more information, realizing instead that he needed to be drawn out of his black mood before it devoured him. "Your mother was lovely," she said cheerfully. "You have her eyes."

"Do you think so?" He smiled slightly in spite of his mysterious thoughts. "I always thought I favored Papa."

She shook her head. "Through the jawline and nose perhaps, but your eyes and your..." Her eyes grazed over his face. "...your lips..." she said quietly, "they are definitely your mother's."

Fredrik's icy gaze clashed with Marie's summery one. He studied her features in silence for a moment, then inclined his head. "Perhaps." Clearing his throat, he reached down inside of his pants and slowly pulled out his thick erection. The head was swollen and already wet with pre-ejaculate. "Come sit on him, *ängel*," he murmured. "Sit on him while we look at the album together."

Marie slithered down from the arm of the chair onto his lap, no longer questioning her sanity for wanting Fredrik, no longer wishing that her body would quit craving his. Her back to his chest, she seated herself slowly, sucking in her breath as the exquisite sensation of her flesh enveloping his became prominent.

He kissed the area of skin from her shoulder to her neck, then flicked out his tongue and made a wet trail up to her ear lobe. Taking the delicate fold of skin into his mouth, he sucked slowly and gently on it, causing her nipples to harden to the point of nearing pain and her breathing to hitch and become shallow.

"Do you like that?" he asked quietly, thickly. "Do you like the feel of my cock inside you and my lips on you?"

"Yes," she whispered, her eyes closed and her head propped back on his shoulder, "I love it."

"Spread your legs wider for me, *ängel*. I want to play with you."

Marie's thighs came open automatically. She shivered when his fingers found her clit, moaned when he rotated his hips and slammed upwards into her slick opening.

"And this is my motorcycle."

Marie's eyelashes batted uncomprehendingly a time or two. Craning her neck, she shot a glance back at Fredrik and snorted at the grin on his face. "There's a time for tripping down memory lane with the aid of one's photo album," she trilled, half teasing and half sexually frustrated. "And then there is a time for creating new memories that are even better than the old ones."

He rubbed her swollen clit and winked. "And which time is this, *ängel*?"

She chuckled and shook her head slightly. "One guess, handsome."

Fredrik's eyes slightly rounded at the term of affection she'd called him by. He hadn't expected something like that from her. Not yet. Not so soon.

He shook off the way the simple endearment melted some of the ice around his façade and reverted back to his previous lighthearted banter. "It's a hell of a motorcycle," he teased, his accent thick, "I haven't ridden her in over ten years, but she's still in perfect condition, sitting in the outside garage waiting for me to return to her."

The light in Marie's eyes faded a bit as her heart broke for him all over again. Ten years. Why did everything come down to that number? It was more than arbitrary she knew, more than a coincidence of fate. He had lost so much, Fredrik had. So incredibly much.

The events surrounding Sophie Anders' death had taken their toll in too many ways. How sad, Marie thought, how poignantly sad that Fredrik hadn't even been able to enjoy such a simple thing as riding his motorcycle throughout the countryside, the wind in his hair, the freedom of such an act something most would take for granted.

An act of self-punishment, she realized. But...why? If he was innocent like she was beginning to suspect, to hope, then why?

"You'll have to take me for a ride sometime," she murmured, her eyes scanning his features. "I would like that very much."

The album fell to the floor forgotten, the pictures like his memories safely sealed away.

The friction on her clit began to intensify as Fredrik's fingers moved in brisk circles about it. She closed her eyes and moaned, then groaned when he rotated his hips and slammed upwards again, seating her fully onto him.

He closed his eyes and smelled the fresh scent of her golden hair. "You are mine," he said possessively against the back of her neck, impaling her onto him once more. "*Bara min* — Only mine."

Chapter 10

Three nights later, her sleep was troubled, though this time not with nightmares of Helena. Rather, it was the sadness she felt for Fredrik that she couldn't seem to let go of long enough to get some peaceful rest, a sadness that had affected her overall mood these past few days and nights.

She found herself tossing and turning, wondering what had driven him to the lonely, reclusive life he lived. Wondering, too, why it had been her of all people that he'd chosen to let inside…if even for a little while.

Marie lay on her side, her gaze staring unblinkingly at the walls, as Fredrik slept soundly beside her. She didn't want to feel anything for him, didn't want to care about him, but conceded that she felt the beginnings of— something. If someone had told her the night Fredrik found her in the forest that a few days later she would be torn as to whether or not she wanted to leave him, she'd have called that person an insane fool.

But now she didn't know. She could no longer make sense of her emotions. The entire situation felt almost surreal and dreamlike to her. As if it was happening to someone else—anyone but Marie Robb.

Anyone but a woman with as many emotional scars as Fredrik bore.

Marie's life growing up had been neither horrible nor idyllic. Her mother had died giving birth to her and her father, while she suspected he loved her, had never been much of a dad. A father, yes, but not a dad—a big difference.

He told her what to do, where to go, whom she could date, whom she was permitted to be friends with…

Always treating her as though she was too simpleminded and fragile to figure these things out for herself. She wouldn't have minded what many called his "overprotectiveness" had he valued her as a worthy person in the process. But, sadly, she knew that respect didn't exist, had never existed.

She was a doll to Paul Robb. Just a pretty doll whose purpose was to smile politely at his business associates, listen to them talk about themselves, and speak only when spoken to. That was it. The whole of her meaning to her father for close to twenty-nine years.

But Fredrik…

He made her feel as though it was possible that a man could care about more than the outside of Marie Robb, as though she was worthy of attention and respect. Odd that she'd found such a foreign feeling at the hands of a reclusive man who had all but kidnapped her to keep her at his side for a week.

She closed her eyes as she relaxed into the silk sheets, fatigue at last getting the best of her. There was so much to think about and yet she found herself not wanting to analyze any of it.

For the remainder of their week together she would simply let life happen. From there, she would see where the path led.

* * * * *

Breakfast was served in the estate's large dining room. Again, Marie had to wonder at how the bounty had appeared, for Fredrik had never left her side to cook it. But there was an entire smorgasbord and, thoughtfully enough, many of her favorite American dishes had been included into it.

She sighed. He was getting to her, Fredrik Sörebo, getting to her and crawling under her skin. Every day drew them closer together, every hour bonded them more in flesh and spirit, every minute forged a new path towards intimacy and friendship.

She had but three days left to make her decision. Three days left and she would be asked to decide the rest of her life. The very thought of it was so heady and consequential that she chose not to dwell on it just yet.

"Where did it come from?" Marie asked as she padded into the room.

Fredrik walked in behind her, fully clothed as always, looking his fill at her naked flesh before absently glancing toward the dining table. He never failed to become erect at the mere sight of her. "Servants." He shrugged his shoulders, dismissing the topic as unimportant.

"And where are they now?" she inquired wide-eyed, not at all liking the idea that one or many of them had perhaps seen her running around nude.

"Gone," he answered, effectively putting her fears to rest. "They won't be back until lunch, *ängel*, so why the worries?"

She lifted a bemused eyebrow. "In case it has escaped your notice, I haven't been allowed to wear clothing in over four days."

His smile was at once sardonic and playful. "That has never once escaped my notice, I assure you."

Marie glanced down toward Fredrik's pants and chuckled when she spied his erection. "I believe you."

"Come take him out," he murmured. "Unzip my pants and take him out."

Her body responded instantaneously to the sound of his words, her nipples tightening as tendrils of sensual need coiled low in her belly.

Grinning, she gazed upward into his eyes. "And what if I say my jaw hurts this morning?" she teased. "Perhaps I'm still too sore from last night." Her voice went down in timbre. "Remember how many times I sucked you off last night?" she whispered, her demeanor evolving from playful to seductive. "Three times as I recall."

"I remember." His tall, muscular form drew closer, slowly closing in on her, as his fingers undid the buttons to his shirt. "You can never get enough, can you?" he asked thickly.

"No." She shook her head slightly, becoming serious for a moment. "Not of you I can't."

"That's good, *ängel*, because I'll never have my fill of you." He came to a halt in front of her, his shirt opened all the way, the black hair of his chest converging downwards until it disappeared in a thin line inside of his pants. "Unzip me, Marie. Take him out and touch him."

He sucked in his breath as she placed her hand over the bulge in his trousers and squeezed. "What am I going to do with him when I take him out?" she murmured. "What does he want this morning, sucked or fucked?"

"Both. But right now he wants held."

Marie's eyes shot up to meet Fredrik's. He was speaking of more than sex and they both knew it. Was he feeling it too, realizing she would have to make a decision soon?

Three days. Just three more days.

Unzipping his pants, Marie watched as his erection sprang loose from the confining material. She wrapped her palm around it and held tightly, then began to slowly masturbate him as she drew her unclothed body into his for an embrace.

They held each other that way for some time, she masturbating him at a leisurely pace while he let his hands roam over her body, feeling every crevice of her flesh.

"I like you naked," he said quietly. "I never want to see clothing on your body again."

Marie chuckled softly, never breaking their intimate embrace. "Not even when we leave the estate? We're bound to do that eventually, you know."

"Hmmm," he playfully replied, "perhaps I'll allow you a fig leaf or two for those rare occasions."

"Two whole fig leaves?" She slid her hand down his erection and palmed his balls, massaging them as she spoke. "You're a big spender I see."

Fredrik laughed at that, causing Marie's heart to tremble a bit. This man rarely smiled let alone laughed outright. But when he did the entire room seemed to light up a bit. His happiness shined better than any amount of candles.

"Come, *ängel*," he said gently as he removed her hand from his body, "let's eat some breakfast before it grows too cold."

"Mmm okay." She smiled up at him, placed a soft kiss in the middle of his chest, then glanced around the dining room.

A golden eyebrow shot up. "There's only one chair, Fredrik." The other brow shot up to meet the first. "I know you're cheap when it comes to clothes," she teased, "but dining room furniture?"

He half-snorted, half-laughed. "I'm sitting on the chair, *ängel*." He waved toward the dining room table. "And you," he said in low tones, his voice thickening with desire, "will sit in front of me on the table."

She shook her head slightly, not understanding. "I will?"

His eyes searched hers. "Come and I'll show you."

A minute later, Marie was seated on the tabletop in front of Fredrik's chair, her buttocks plopped down onto the middle of his place setting, her thighs spread wide open, her labia and clit on glistening display.

Fredrik fed her from his plate with one hand while the other massaged the tiny and aroused piece of flesh between her legs. Within minutes, she was well sated in terms of appetite, but still hungry in other ways.

Opening her legs wider, she rotated her hips upward to meet his palm and fingers. "Rub me a bit faster, Fredrik," she said as her breathing hitched. "I'm so close it's agony."

"Not just yet, *ängel*."

She grunted. "Why?"

He chuckled, his fingers still softly rimming her clit and labia. "Because it's time for me...to eat." His gaze caught hers and held it.

Marie's body stilled as she considered what he was trying to tell her in so many words. Her nipples hardened and elongated as she figured it out. "And you want me to feed you?" she softly inquired.

"Mmmm. Yes, *ängel*."

She eyed the covered dishes arranged to the left of her, then turned her head back to look at Fredrik. "And what are you hungry for?"

He took a deep breath as he glanced toward the culinary selections. "Something simple, I think. I'm in the mood for fruit."

A golden eyebrow arched up. "Strawberries, perhaps?"

"Strawberries would be divine."

Placing her hand in a bowl of ripe fruit, she withdrew two plump strawberries and held them in her palm. She smiled at Fredrik, then spent the next several moments fitting the berries over her nipples. She was so turned on that the task wasn't at all difficult, her elongated nipples gliding easily inside the middle of the succulent fruit bits, which she'd carved out with the tip of a knife.

When she was finished, she reached for a banana and dangled it coyly before Fredrik. "Care for a slice?"

He grinned. "Goes well with strawberries."

"Mmm." Quickly cutting up a few chucky slices, Marie placed the first piece just outside the entrance to her vagina, then shoved it up inside of her with two fingers. She was wet and warm inside, inducing the fruit to slide in rather easily. She did the same with two more slices of banana before pronouncing herself ready.

She smiled as she lay down on her back, spreading her thighs wide as she reclined. "Breakfast is served," she giggled, blushing slightly in spite of herself.

"Mmm. My very favorite."

And then his tongue was wrapping around the first strawberry, toying with it, teasing it, removing it from her nipple and sucking on the berry even as he sucked on her nipple simultaneously. Marie forgot all about being shy. She sucked in her breath and closed her eyes.

"Don't forget the other strawberry," she whispered. "It's as ripe as the first one was."

"Patience, *ängel*." Fredrik's tongue made a trail from the first nipple, down into her cleavage, up the swell of her other breast, and wrapped around the second strawberry. Popping it in his mouth, he took her nipple between his teeth and suckled vigorously at it.

"Oh my God," she breathed out.

"*Mmm*." He released the nipple a minute later, a slight popping sound echoing in the dining room as he did so. "It will get even better," he promised.

He flicked at her nipple with his tongue a few times in rapid succession, then trailed kisses from her breast down to her belly. He toyed with her navel a bit, waited until he felt Marie squirm beneath him, then meandered further down, his lips forging a trail toward her wet flesh.

"Bananas," he murmured. "Smells heavenly. I wonder how I'll get to them?"

Marie's breathing grew shallow, realizing of course, that there was only one way to do so. "I'm sure you'll figure something out," she breathed.

"This perhaps?" His lips found her flesh as he darted his tongue deep inside of her. He swirled it around a few times, enjoying her reaction, appreciating the way her hips writhed for him.

"Not quite," she groaned.

Fredrik removed his tongue from inside of her and pretended to ponder the matter over. "Hmm," he said, tapping his cheek, his English heavily accented, "if sliding my tongue inside of that sweet pussy doesn't work, then what will?"

Marie closed her eyes briefly, her breaths coming in short pants. "Try sucking it out."

"Sucking?"

"Yes."

"Like…"the playful edge to his voice died abruptly, replaced with desire and need, "…this?"

In one forceful movement, Fredrik's face dived downwards, his mouth, tongue, and lips covering her entire center. He sucked hard on her clit, slurping sounds resonating throughout the dining room, as he laved her with his tongue and mouth.

"Oh God yes."

Marie's hips flared upwards, grinding her clit and labia more forcefully against his mouth. *"Fredrik, yes."*

He sucked on her flesh for a few more moments, then the pad of his thumb replaced his mouth as he trailed a path down with his lips and covered the entrance to her vagina. Sucking lustily, his thumb rubbed her clit in brisk circles as his mouth suctioned the fruit from her flesh.

"*Oh yes! Oh God! Oh yes!*"

Her hips thrashing upwards, Marie's entire body convulsed as she surrendered to the pleasure and climaxed. Moaning, her head fell back against the tabletop as she came, her nipples stabbing up and her face heating with rushing blood.

"Fredrik," she whispered, panting heavily for air, "oh Fredrik that was…*oh God.*"

He impaled her in one fluid motion, now standing on his feet before her splayed out body. Grabbing her hips, he pulled her closer to the table's edge and began to thrust in and out of her in long, deep strokes.

"*Ja, min ängel,*" he rasped out, his jaws clenched, "your pussy feels so good to me."

"Faster," she pleaded. "I need it faster."

"Wrap your legs around me, beautiful one."

Marie complied instantly, arching her hips up to meet his thrusts as she wrapped her legs around his waist. Groaning, she closed her eyes and let her head fall back down on the tabletop as she enjoyed the sensations elicited by Fredrik's lovemaking.

"*Harder.*"

He picked up the pace of his thrusting, the sound of her wet flesh enveloping his steel-hard shaft over and over slapping throughout the room. "Open your eyes, *ängel,*" he said possessively. "Open your eyes and see who it is that brings you to pleasure."

Half-moaning and half-panting, Marie tried to comply but couldn't. All she could do was feel, enjoy, experience.

Fredrik clamped down on her nipples with his thumbs and forefingers even as he continued to ride her flesh hard. "I said open them," he commanded. "Open your eyes, *ängel*, and see me."

"*Oh God.*"

Marie's eyes flew open and locked with Fredrik's as an intense orgasm ripped through her belly. She heard his words of encouragement through the haze of desire, knew he was telling her that she belonged to him, before she closed her eyes once more and screamed from the pleasure.

Fredrik held onto her nipples as he thrust deeply into her once, twice, three times more. His breathing labored, he gritted his teeth and threw his head back as his body began to convulse. "Marie. *God – Marie.*" Muscles cording, he shouted out her name as he spurted his orgasm deep inside of her.

Some moments later, when they'd both come down enough from their mutually experienced high to speak, Marie wiggled her hips, emphasizing the fact that they were still joined. Exhausted, she half-laughed and half-groaned. "I don't think he wants to leave me just yet."

"He doesn't want to leave you ever," Fredrik amended, smiling down at her.

One of her eyebrows shot up teasingly. "And your fingers? Do they plan to clutch my nipples forever?" She glanced down to her chest where her erect nipples remained clamped between his thumbs and forefingers.

He chuckled. "I love your nipples." He lowered his head long enough to flick his tongue across the peaks.

Growing serious, his head came up and his smile waned. "Why let go of something you love?" he asked meaningfully, his voice having gone down in timbre.

Marie's eyes shot up to meet his gaze. She didn't speak for a drawn-out moment, just studied his facial features and the intense look about him.

At last she spoke, her voice barely a whisper. "I'm beginning to ask myself the same question." She smiled slowly. "Why indeed."

He breathed in deeply, then exhaled slowly. "I love you, Marie."

"Fredrik, I—"

"Shh." He released one of her nipples and gently placed two fingers over her lips. "You don't have to say anything, *ängel*. Just know that it's true."

Marie closed her eyes, too overwhelmed to hold his gaze. After a few moments she nodded, inducing Fredrik to remove his hand from her mouth.

"Thank you," she whispered, her eyes finding his once more. "Thank you."

Part III:
The Choice

Chapter 11

Marie smiled at the sound of Fredrik's humming as it wafted through the closed bathroom door and permeated the atmosphere of the bedroom. He always did that when he shaved, a boyishly endearing quality.

"I'm cold," she muttered to herself as she padded toward the bedroom's walk-in closet. "Like it or not, handsome, I'm borrowing one of your shirts."

Doing a little humming herself, she threw open the closet doors and strolled inside. Glancing around, she quickly decided that the man had a definite affinity towards the color black.

Black coats, black trousers, black shoes, black boots...there was little variance to relieve the harshness of it, save one or two white silk shirts.

Good lord, Fredrik, she smiled to herself. *I like wearing black, too, but this is almost morbid.* She ran her hands over two black greatcoats, then made a part between them. Her gaze landed on a small table filled with watches and the like sitting just behind the coats, causing her smile to falter a bit.

What's this? she mentally asked herself. Marie squinted her eyes a bit to compensate for the closet's dull light. Drawing her head closer, her body stilled completely when her gaze settled upon one object in particular.

"My barrette," she murmured, reaching out to clasp the piece of jewelry in her hand. "The barrette I lost back in..."

Her eyes widened as comprehension dawned. God in heaven, she thought in horror, please say it wasn't possible that...

Oh God.

Her breathing quickly growing labored, Marie wracked her brain to find the answer she sought. Her hair had come undone and her barrette had fallen to the ground sometime during her walk in the woods that night the Saab had acquired the flat tire. And if she wasn't mistaken, she had lost it rather early on, almost from the beginning of that hours-long trek through the forest.

How could Fredrik have found it unless…unless he had been there the entire time, watching from a distance as she had stumbled around in circles, tired and afraid?

"He killed her." Helena's parched lips turned upward, forming a cruel slash of a smile. *"Raped her and murdered her. Cut her into pieces and threw her to the dogs."*

Marie's hand reflexively flew up to cover her mouth. She balled it into a fist and bit down on it.

Oh God no.

"He'll do the same to you. If you allow him near you, the same will become of you."

Her breaths coming in short gasps, she stilled completely, listening for the sounds of Fredrik's humming, proof that he was still in the bathroom and not about to walk in on her and realize she'd found the barrette.

Mozart. He was humming one of Mozart's compositions.

Closing her eyes, she took a deep breath and exhaled, then went about the business of quickly dressing herself into Fredrik's clothes.

She didn't have time. No time. He would finish soon. He would come for her. And he would know. He always knew. Yes, Marie thought hysterically, he always knew.

Slapping a belt around her waist to hold up the trousers, she unthinkingly threw the barrette down onto the ground, desperate to get away while she still had a chance. Before he got to her and…oh God, what would he do?

She had no time to consider the rashness of her actions, no time to worry about whether or not she was jumping to unfounded conclusions. Later she could think all she wanted. Later, when she was safe. Later, when she was still…alive.

For now, she didn't care. All she understood in the here and now was the primal need for survival, for continuing on at all costs.

Sucking in her breath to hold back the tears of anger, fright, and disappointment, she tiptoed quietly toward the entrance to the bedroom, made certain he was still in the bathroom unawares, then sprinted at top speed down the twisting staircase that led to the ground floor below.

Buttoning up his shirt to conceal her naked breasts, she flew through the front door and ran into the forest as fast as her legs would carry her.

"I'm sorry, Fredrik," she whispered to the trees, "but being with you is a chance I can no longer take."

* * * * *

Fredrik sat on the edge of the bed, his head hung low. He twirled the black barrette absently between his fingers as he stared at nothing. The muscles in his back corded and tensed, the power of his emotions so raw and all consuming.

She was gone. Marie was gone.

He should have told her the truth. From the beginning. He should have told her everything.

About Sophie. About Helena. About that black night ten years past. About what had really happened.

And he should have admitted that he'd lured Marie into the woods as well. And then he should have admitted why.

Because…he needed her.

Because he connected with her. Because from the first moment he'd laid eyes on her, he had…*felt*.

He'd been dead inside so long. So incredibly long. Stark. Barren. An abyss.

And then along came Marie Robb. The beautiful woman with the large eyes and a wounded heart as buried as his own. He had looked into her eyes and he had known. Somehow, in some inexplicable manner, he had known she was the one that would bring light back into the dark void.

But now that light was gone, and all that remained was the blackness.

He should have told her.

Why, he asked himself, as he ran a punishing hand through his short dark hair, why had he not confided in her this entire last week? Why had he let her go on believing the worst without offering her the truth?

Fredrik took a deep breath as he hoisted himself to his feet. Glancing about the bedroom, he closed his eyes against the pain.

The bed linens smelled of her scent. The walls echoed her laughter.

The sound of her climaxing in his arms. The smug look on her face when she beat him at chess. The serenity of her expression when she painted…

"Christ," he murmured, his hand balling into a fist. "Christ."

Chapter 12
The Scottish Highlands
One Month Later

Marie nibbled on her lower lip as she touched the paintbrush to canvas and tried once more to recreate the majestic autumn scenery surrounding her. There was nothing quite so lovely, so breathtaking, as the lush green forests of the Highlands woven with brightly vivid flowers and fauna of varying colors.

She sighed, closing her eyes briefly. It wasn't working. And worse yet, she knew why. Something, or rather *someone*, was missing from the equation.

Fredrik.

The stone cottage she'd purchased to live out the rest of her life in was exactly what she'd always wanted. It was neither too small nor too large, neither too isolated nor smack-dab in the middle of a city.

The serene little cottage was located in a remote area of Scotland, ideal for when she wanted to be alone, yet close enough to the city of Inverness for when she needed to be around other people.

And what's more, she was finally in charge of her own destiny. She was finally all grown up. She'd taken extreme relish in telling her father that she wasn't returning to the States...ever. And that she would see him...perhaps never again.

It hadn't been a difficult decision to make, not once she'd set her eyes on this terrific little stone fortress, this cottage that called to her on so many levels.

Marie had found peace here, an inner serenity, a sense of well-being she'd never again sacrifice for anyone. She would never return to the States again, not even to visit.

And yet as happy as she was in the Highlands, she was also fundamentally aware of the fact that something important was missing here—a man. But not just any man, of course. Not just any man would do. She missed Fredrik.

Fredrik Sörebo. Marie shook her head and sighed as she set the paintbrush in a dish of cleaner and absently stared at her painting.

Why did she miss him? she asked herself for the umpteenth time since leaving Göthmoor. He was secretive and mysterious, dominant and unbending, authoritative and…

She frowned as she raked a hand through her mane of golden hair. There was no use trying to talk herself out of it. No matter Fredrik's faults, she knew the man that dwelled beneath them. She knew he was intrinsically honest, fundamentally loyal and devout.

Those things Helena had said weren't true. They couldn't be true. They simply didn't add up.

It no longer mattered to her what Fredrik's role had been in that tragedy ten years past because she knew he hadn't done the horrific things he'd been accused of. It simply wasn't possible.

Guilt stabbed through her as she admitted to herself for the first time since she'd left Göthmoor that she had known the truth before she'd run from him. Even before then she had known it. And yet like a coward, as afraid of her emotions as she'd once been of Fredrik, she had still run away.

"What have I done?" she whispered to herself. "Damn it, what have I done?"

And it got worse. Marie closed her eyes and took a cathartic breath as she contemplated just how much worse it actually got.

Fredrik had been looking for her, she knew. She had been tracked down as far as Inverness several times by him, but he'd gotten no further. He must have left Scotland altogether, for he'd left a letter behind for her with one of the solicitors in town, probably never expecting her to receive it. Indeed, the fact that she had received it had been a fluke, a coincidence that had taken her to that same lawyer to ask his advice on some trivial visa problems.

The letter was here, in her cottage. The letter from Fredrik that she had never read, that she had thrown in a drawer and refused to so much as glance at for fear that it would cause her to feel as badly about what she'd done to him as she felt this very moment.

Groaning, she hoisted herself up to her feet and made a beeline for the cottage door. "You're an idiot, Marie," she chastised herself through clenched teeth. "An idiot."

She found the letter precisely where she'd left it, sitting in an unused drawer within the stone cottage's airy kitchen. She fumbled to get the envelope open and remove the letter it concealed. Closing her eyes, she held the parchment up to her nose and breathed in the scent.

Fredrik.

She would have known by the musky, masculine scent alone that the letter had been written by him.

Her heart pounding, she fell into the chair closest to her standing position and began to read.

My Dearest Marie:

I don't blame you for running, so don't think that I do. So many unanswered questions, so many things I could have said to make you understand what had happened so long ago, and yet I held my silence.

I've asked myself why for weeks now and all I can come up with is that I didn't want to take the chance of losing you, to have you know what had happened that night and decide against Us.

And yet, this is precisely what has happened, has it not? Life can be decidedly ironic.

I didn't kill, Sophie, ängel. Or at least not on purpose. I loved the girl once, or thought I did at the time.

She was young and she was beautiful and she was full of life, Sophie was. But there was a dark side to her as well. An emptiness and a void that eventually overpowered her and became all-consuming. It was a side of her I hadn't been shown until the day she died.

Marie's eyes widened as she scanned the pages. She was about to find out what happened. So much gossip, so many questions, and finally she was about to be told the truth of that horrific night ten years past. She clutched the letter tighter, crinkling the edges.

Before her death, Sophie had come to me, wanting to confide in me, but was afraid I would turn away from her if I knew the truth. I assured her that was not the case, that it would never be the case, that she could tell me anything and I'd never leave her. I've heard it said that one should be careful before making such blanket statements and I was soon to discover how true those words rang.

Sophie, you see, was pregnant. And I knew the child couldn't possibly be mine because we had never consummated our relationship. So when she came to me at the estate and found me out on the balcony, I turned on her. I flew into a rage and turned on her. I didn't touch her, mind you, but merely shouted at her.

I didn't care what promises I'd made, didn't care about anything else other than the fact that she had given her body to another man. And worse, she had given her body to another man yet had never allowed me to touch her.

I wanted her out of my house, gone from my sight. I yelled at her to leave, to never come back. She was just like all the others before her, I'd shouted. A lying little slut that would tell a man anything to get what she wanted from him. A betrayer who wanted me for my money and nothing else.

But then when she turned to leave, I felt a sudden sense of guilt and sadness. I quieted down and held out my hand to her, telling her not to go, to come back out to the balcony and that we would speak of what had happened together.

I thought she would be relieved, grateful even. But she wasn't. When she turned around she was...smiling. Literally...smiling.

I'll never forget the eerie look in her eyes, the upward tilt to her lips as she slowly turned around to face me. It was enough to make me wary, a tad frightened even. That I stood a foot taller and eighty pounds heavier didn't even register.

"You're a fool, Fredrik," she had said. "A bloody fool. Did you honestly think I would ever let an ugly creature like you touch me when there are so many others much more handsome to choose from?"

"Oh Fredrik," Marie whispered, a single tear tracking slowly down her cheek. "She was wrong. So very wrong."

And then Sophie told me the name of the man she'd been lying with, the name of the man who had taken her to his bed, made her climax repeatedly, and had gotten her with child. She told me his name and I thought I was going to become ill, Marie. So I shouted at her to go, to leave once and for all because the very sight of her made my skin crawl.

That's when Sophie lost it completely. She lunged at me like some sort of rabid animal, clawing at me with her nails and spewing all sorts of vile things.

I didn't know how to react really. I wasn't certain what to do. But my reflexes took over and I pushed her away from me with all of the force in my body.

And then, like something out of a bad movie, I watched in horror as the balcony railing gave way and Sophie began to lose her balance. In that moment she looked sane again. In that moment she had become rational long enough to realize that she was going to die, that she was falling and that she was going to die.

"Fredrik!" She had screamed, holding her hand out to me.

And I swear to you, Marie, I swear to you that I lunged for her and tried to make it in time. And had I been closer to her I might have made it.

But I wasn't…and I didn't.

Sophie fell from the balcony and there was nothing I could do to save her. I heard her scream throughout the duration of the entire fifty-foot plummet. The very sound of it, the sound a person makes when they know they are dying…I hear it in my nightmares to this day.

Marie clamped a hand over her mouth.

She fell until her body hit an area of jagged rocks on the beach below. She hit it with such force that her chest was impaled by an oblong stone, leaving behind a hole the size of a basketball.

For hours I sat there on the precipice of the broken ledge, too in shock, too horrified to do anything else. I should have gone and cleaned up her remains that Helena might have had at least that.

But I simply sat there instead, hours flying by like minutes, as wild dogs fed from the broken flesh of a young girl who lay dead on a pile of jagged rocks, her body impregnated by her own father…

"Oh my God."

Marie's heart clenched as she read the remainder of the story. She hated herself in that moment for not having stood by Fredrik, despised herself for giving credence even a second long to what the obviously crazed Helena had said about him.

And then the story of Sophie Anders' death ended and the letter continued, Fredrik then having recounted the last ten years of his life for her, telling her of the guilt and shame that had consumed him for so long.

And finally he spoke of her, of Marie, and the tears began to flow.

You did as I requested and gave me a week of your life. A week to walk in the sunshine with you. A week to feel like a whole man again. A week to fall in love and have the pleasure of getting to know the real Marie Robb. I did all of those things and more, ängel…

Marie swiped at her eyes with the sleeve of her art smock. Her hands were shaking so badly she had to set the letter on the kitchen tabletop and hover over it to finish.

I will never forget not even one moment of the time we spent together. Never.

I will remember each laugh, each embrace, each climax, each smile.

When first I saw you I had determined to keep you. I thought never to give you the choice to leave me for I wanted you that much.

But the more time I spent with you, the more I fell in love with you, and the more I began to realize that I couldn't do it. Not and then attempt afterward to live in peace with myself.

You've been like a caged bird all of your life, ängel, singing to everybody's tune but your own. Papa's tune. Society's tune. Even my tune. But never to Marie's.

I hope you have found whatever it is you were looking for in Scotland, ängel, and I hope you're singing a song that for once belongs only to you.

And yet I also hope you will think back on our week from time to time and remember it kindly. And whenever the nights grow cold and lonely, remember that there is a man in Sweden who carries you in his heart always.

Thank you, min ängel. *Thank you for everything you've given to me. I will hold it close to my heart and cherish it always.*

Now go paint pretty pictures and sing happy songs and never again let any fool tell you that your love of doing so isn't worthwhile.

You said to me once that I am worthy. Well Marie, ängel, *so too are you. Never doubt it.*

All of my love,

Fredrik

Chapter 13

Fredrik studied the portrait Marie had painted of him standing amongst his gardens as he sipped from his morning cup of coffee. The gardens in question were full of life today, vibrant blooms of color contrasted against an equally alive sky.

He ran a callused finger over one painted flower, a bud Marie had painted into the picture that had yet to bloom. "Sort of like me, *ängel*, before I'd met you."

Smiling nostalgically, he removed his finger from the portrait and absently stared out into the gardens as he continued to sip from his coffee. He wondered what Marie was doing this very moment, wondered if she thought about him from time to time, or even at all.

For her, he realized, more than a month had passed by, wherein her memories of him had perhaps faded somewhat. But for him, for Fredrik, he still felt caught up in the middle of their week in paradise, replaying each moment over and over again in his mind until he became too grief stricken to continue.

To do it all over again, he would have told her the truth from the beginning. Or if not from the beginning then close enough to it. He had let guilt from the way Sophie had died and gossip of villagers drive him into solitude. Once upon a time he hadn't minded it so much. But then once upon a time he hadn't known Marie.

He missed her. Christ how he —

"Hello, Fredrik."

He stilled. Shocked, and not altogether certain that he wasn't imagining things, he drew his head up slowly and looked around, visually scanning the garden.

Nobody.

Jesus, he truly was losing it.

Sighing, Fredrik set down his coffee cup and stood up to leave. The gardens...there were simply too many memories of her here. He needed to leave this place, and preferably before he lost his mind altogether.

"I said hello, Fredrik."

Fredrik's head shot up as he scanned the gardens once more. That time he was certain he'd heard a woman's voice...and that just maybe he'd heard *her* voice.

And then she emerged from one of the paths and his heart rate increased by tenfold. She was naked, completely naked, just as she'd been during their entire week in the sun.

"Marie," he murmured.

She smiled slowly, coming to a halt before him when she reached his side. She nodded. "I'm here," she whispered.

Stunned and overwhelmed, he could only scan her features, memorizing every line, every curve, and committing them to memory. At last, after many moments had been spent in silence, he shook his head slightly and met her gaze. "But why?" he asked somewhat shakily. "Why did you come back?"

Marie smiled up at him, her eyes glistening with unshed tears. "I came to take you home," she said softly.

Those words. The very same words Fredrik had said to her all those weeks past...

Closing his eyes, he sucked in his breath to steady himself, not wanting to appear weak before Marie.

"I love you, Fredrik," she whispered, her hand reaching out to unzip his trousers. "I love you and I've come to take you home."

And then he no longer cared whether a stray tear or two ran unchecked, for he had Marie in his arms and her flesh was welcoming his as they took to the grass and made love in the sun.

He impaled her over and over, again and again, never wanting the moment to stop, never wanting the feeling to end. She clung to him with all of her body, all of her emotions, her legs wrapped tightly around his waist, her throat bared to his mouth as he thrust deeply inside of her.

Some minutes later when they lay spent and replete in each other's arms, Fredrik gathered her as tightly against him as possible and squeezed her affectionately.

"You said you were going to take me home," he whispered in low tones, his voice husky from their lovemaking.

"I am."

"For how long will you keep me?" he asked seriously.

Marie searched his clear blue gaze and smiled contently. "Forever and a day," she murmured. "Forever and a day."

Part IV:
Phoenix From The Flames

Epilogue

Marie laughed as she wrapped her arms around Fredrik's waist and held on tightly. "I've never ridden on a motorcycle naked before!" she yelled in order to be heard over the noise of the engine.

"Neither have I!" he shouted back, laughing as the wind whipped about them. "It's pretty cool."

Marie grinned, loving how he picked up American phrases of hers and unthinkingly threw them into sentences. "I wonder if we'll be able to find any roads to do this on when we get to the Highlands next week!"

Fredrik shrugged his shoulders and chuckled. "We'll make a new road together if one doesn't already exist." He glanced back at her long enough to wink.

Marie squeezed him around the middle and placed a kiss on the back of his neck. He was speaking in double entendres again, only this time she knew precisely what he'd meant. "Fredrik?"

"Hm?"

"*Jag älskar dig.*"

He smiled fully, displaying a line of neat white teeth. "*Ja*, baby. I love you too."

TREMORS

JAID BLACK

THE OBSESSION

To Dr. Zelling, for putting the ghosts to rest…

Prologue I
Edinburgh, Scotland

"Good morning, Margaret." Dr. Neil Macalister formally inclined his head, offering his arm to the woman he'd been dating for approximately two months. Escorting her to a middle pew in Blackfriar Kirk's sanctuary, he settled into the seat beside her and awaited the deliverance of the Sunday sermon.

Quietly clearing her throat, Margaret smiled as she offered him a stick of gum. "Would you care for a piece?" She blushed, growing nervous when he turned to regard her through his wire-rimmed spectacles. "I-It's your favorite," she stammered out.

Neil slowly smiled, his brown eyes crinkling at the corners. "Thank you. That was thoughtful of you, my dear." He accepted the stick of gum and popped it into his mouth. Chewing quietly, he turned his attention back toward the front of the sanctuary where even now the minister was making his way to the podium.

As the sermon began, Neil found his thoughts straying to the woman beside him. Margaret was desirous of marriage, he knew, and truth be told Neil had reached the stage in life where he no longer cared to be alone. He was thirty-nine, almost forty, could claim no children, and had never been wed. So for what was at least the fifth time in the past two weeks he allowed himself to consider the merits behind a union with Margaret.

Companionship. Mutual respect. Similar upbringings. And Margaret was a fine cook to boot. She would make for a brilliant housewife and a terrific mother to his future children. He wished he held no qualms whatsoever in regards to marriage, but he supposed a touch of cold feet was to be expected.

Margaret was rather ordinary of face and form, neither ugly nor beautiful. She was timid and reserved by nature, preferring to defer to Neil in all things. There was nothing particularly exciting about Margaret or her life, her idea of a good time being dinner over at her mum's every Sunday following worship services. But Neil didn't mind.

Neil was a sensible man not given to flights of fancy or passionate exchanges. A university lecturer of mathematics, he was authoritative and a tad brusque, dealing better with numbers than with people. Margaret understood these things about him and tolerated him for what he was. In return, he tolerated her affection for the church, not being an overly religious sort himself.

In so much that Margaret was a tad humdrum, so too was Neil. He wasn't the sort of man one puts on a guest list in the hopes of livening up a dull party, but rather, he was the sort of man one calls upon when they have a flat tire and are in need of a ride to work. He was reliable and dependable, the very attributes that assured him he'd make Margaret a most proper husband.

When the sermon came to an end, Neil rose to his feet and ushered Margaret towards her car. She clung to his arm, blushing slightly at the intimate feel of his muscles bulging beneath her hand. "I had a terrific time. I thought the sermon quite good. Did you?" she asked hopefully.

Neil nodded his agreement. "I particularly enjoyed the minister's recitation on the book of Daniel. I thought his insight remarkable."

"Indeed," Margaret demurred, "I can only agree."

He smiled.

When they reached her vehicle, she handed him the keys and waited while he unlocked the car door for her. "Will I see you at Mum's this afternoon?" She released his arm and smiled demurely. "She's preparing all your favorite dishes."

Neil rubbed his belly and grinned. "How can I pass up so tempting an offer? Of course I'll be there, Margaret."

Her blush grew deeper. "I'll see you at two then."

"At two it is."

Neil watched as Margaret's sensible four-door sedan made a turn out of Blackfriar Kirk's parking lot and into traffic. She truly was all things practical and reliable, characteristics that were manifested in everything from her conservative no-frills attire to her clean but modest car.

He supposed he already knew what his decision should be. Neil was, after all, a most sensible man.

Prologue II
Atlanta, Georgia

"Take it off, baby! Take it off!"

"That's right honey! Hell yeah!"

Valentina Jason-Elliot laughed at her best friends' antics. She watched in amused delight as Cynthia and Holly jumped up out of their seats and stuffed five dollar bills down an almost naked male stripper's g-string. The stripper, who went by the stage name Hang Twelve, looked as though he lived up to his reputation. He winked at the women, grinning audaciously as they oohed and aahed over the bulge in his metallic silver undergarment. Valentina dissolved into a fit of giggles.

"What's so funny?" Cynthia settled back into her seat and grinned as she picked up her glass of Chardonnay.

Valentina smiled. "From Holly I've come to expect the outrageous, but from you?" She shook her head and chuckled. "Too funny."

Cynthia saluted her with the glass of wine. "When the cat's away..." She let her sentence trail off playfully, wiggling her eyebrows like Groucho Marx. She knew Valentina would never judge her or think anything of the fact that a woman married twelve years was indulging in a little harmless fun on a night out with her single friends.

Indeed, Valentina had long been considered the freethinker of their group, which was saying a lot for two writers and an artist. Born to hippie parents who believed in everything from free love to the legalization of marijuana, very little had been considered taboo while growing up.

In her early twenties, Valentina had dabbled in everything from lesbian sex to spending the occasional weekend getaway at nude resorts such as Jamaica's famous *Hedonism*. She'd dated men of different cultures, men of different social strata, and because of that fact she was very comfortable and assured of what made her tick.

Unlike the friends of her acquaintance, Valentina's parents had actually encouraged her to try new things, to experiment sexually that she might find what worked for her and what didn't. They'd lectured her severely to be careful, to always take precaution against diseases, but they'd encouraged her nonetheless. A fact that had made her family life seem quite idyllic and trendy amongst her peers while growing up.

In truth, her life had been no more idyllic than anyone else's. Her family had experienced the same ups and downs, joys and sorrows, as any other family. They'd just been more open with each other about the taboo than what was probably considered normal.

Now twenty-nine and getting closer to the big three-o, she knew what she wanted, had a firm grasp on her libido and its needs. She no longer had the drive to experiment, hadn't had such an urge in over three years in fact, for she was very much in touch with her desires.

And what she desired more than anything else, she'd realized a little over a month ago, was an exclusive, monogamous relationship with a man as adventurous as she was. A man who puts the F in Fun, a man who could snag her attention and keep it.

She didn't want a boring, reliable geek like the man Cynthia was married to. Osmond was a nice man she supposed, but dull, dull, dull. No, she wanted something vastly different for herself. She wanted a man who would whisk her away on a moment's notice for a diving trip to

Micronesia, take her to all of the latest gallery exhibits of her favorite artists, fly her to Paris on a whim and hold her captive there for a week or two while they made love and drank wine.

Osmond's idea of adventurous, Cynthia had complained to her, was dinner out at the local steak house, and if she was really lucky, a movie afterwards. Definitely not what Valentina was looking for.

Valentina good-naturedly blamed her inability to settle for the ordinary on her far from ordinary parents. They heralded from the Age of Aquarius, from a moment in time when passion had ruled over logic. And Valentina had followed in their footsteps in more ways than one.

Her mother was a performance artist, her father an equally talented playwright. By the age of ten, Valentina had known she would follow their lead, and indeed, like her father, she had become a writer. Where her father wrote for Broadway, however, she wrote strictly suspense novels. She hadn't quite reached the level of notoriety her parents had, but she was firmly on her way.

"So," Cynthia asked, her attention now trained on Valentina since the pulsating noise of the music and the strobe lights from the stage were winding down until the next act, "how long will you be gone to that art festival?"

"Which one?" Holly said wryly.

Cynthia chuckled. "The overseas one. That festival in Edinburgh."

Valentina smiled, her light green eyes twinkling. "A month. The festival is *the* grandest in Europe I'm told. I can't wait to see it."

Cynthia nodded. "Is this just another working holiday or a real honest-to-goodness, full-fledged vacation?"

"I guess you could say both." She picked up her White Russian and swirled it around in the glass. "Ballast

Books is throwing a couple of parties there in an effort to introduce their writers to the European market. But for the most part, the month is my own."

"Lucky girl."

"Yeah." She smiled. "You guys wanna come?" She looked pointedly at Cynthia. "You're supposed to be there anyway. You are a Ballast writer if you will recall."

Cynthia snorted at that. "Os would never let me leave for an entire month, girl. He'd never watch Erica while I was gone. You know that."

Holly sighed. "It's a no-go for me too. I've got two exhibits scheduled next month."

"I'm sorry I'll miss them," Valentina said sincerely. "I wish I'd known about them before I went and prepaid for the entire month's trip."

Holly waved that away. "I understand. Besides, I haven't left my Black Period yet," she said dramatically. "The pieces I'll be exhibiting are all new ones, but nothing drastically altered from my last showing in Manhattan."

Valentina nodded. "I love your Black Period. Very smoky and sexy." Smiling slowly, she tilted her head toward Cynthia. "And if you change your mind and can get away, if even for a few days, come on over. I've already got the hotel room, all you need are the plane tickets."

Cynthia smiled, loving the idea. "Thank you. If I can arrange it, I'll be there!"

Valentina didn't respond because the music was picking back up and a new performer dressed up like Darth Vader was taking to the stage. Besides, there was no point in responding. Cynthia would never show up in Edinburgh and they both knew it. Cynthia would never do anything to rock the boat at home in order to gain a few days of paradise sans Osmond. Cynthia was a most sensible woman, a woman not given to flights of fancy or momentary whims.

Nothing at all like Valentina.

Chapter 1
Edinburgh, Scotland
Two Weeks Later

"It really isn't necessary to purchase me a new pair of trousers, Neil." Margaret smiled up to him as they entered Jenners Department Store. "I realize you didn't mean to spill that glass of juice on my tweed suit. Truly, the stain can probably still be worked out."

"It's no bother, Margaret." He inclined his head as they made their way toward the women's section. "I soiled a perfectly good pair of trousers with my clumsiness and I feel it only proper that I replace them."

"How kind of you," she demurred.

Neil made no comment as they neared a rack of chic designer dresses. A voluptuous woman of medium height stood an aisle over, her blood-red nails leafing through the various selections. Her hand stilled on a black, barely there Calvin Klein dress, then her fingers slowly ran over the material to test the feel of it beneath her skin.

The blood-red nails made their selection, picking up the scant piece of black material. The woman disappeared as quickly as she'd been spotted, and Neil found himself oddly curious as to what she had looked like. From his vantage point, he had seen only a tanned hand and a set of long, crimson-tipped nails. Clothing racks had blocked the rest.

"These dresses are all rubbish." Margaret's lips pinched together disapprovingly. "The sort of clothing a street walker might don."

It occurred to Neil that her source of upset was a particularly classy display of Donna Karan's, but he held his tongue. Margaret was, after all, a conservative dresser. "I believe the trousers are two aisles over." He took her by the elbow and led her in the right direction. "I trust you'll find something suitable over here."

"Ah yes. Now this is more like it." Upon reaching their destination, Margaret picked up a pair of camel tweed trousers and smiled. "This pair is rather fetching, don't you agree?"

Neil mentally winced. Though he found the boring brown tweeds anything but riveting, he declined to mention as much. Margaret was entitled to dress as she saw fit. Not to mention the fact that the trousers might look vastly different on her from how they appeared on the rack.

Besides, Neil reminded himself, he oftentimes wore formal tweed trousers to lecture in. The socially backwards Neanderthal in him, however, wished the woman he'd been courting had a care for more feminine-looking apparel.

"Excellent." He smiled. "Would you care to try them on? To see if they fit?"

She bit her lip. "You don't mind waiting?" she asked hesitantly.

Inwardly, Neil sighed. On one hand, he knew enough about himself and his dominant personality to realize he didn't outright object to Margaret's constant deferment to him, but on the other hand, it sometimes aggravated him that she was so timid she feared for expressing her opinions at all. A quandary, that. And not one he cared to dwell upon just now. "Not at all."

Ten minutes later, Neil checked his watch, wondering how long it could possibly take to try on a pair of tweed trousers. But he was a patient man, so he stood outside the women's try-on area without so much as a grumble. A few seconds later, he heard the door to the changing room open. He glanced up, assuming it was Margaret. It wasn't.

A tanned hand and blood-red nails emerged first, causing Neil's heart rate to inexplicably pick up. The attractively polished hand opened the door all the way, revealing a beautiful woman who sported light brown hair with golden highlights dressed in a black, barely there Calvin Klein dress.

A man of science, it didn't escape Neil's notice that the closer the woman walked toward him, the faster his heart rate picked up. He'd never felt such an elemental, primal response to a woman. The sheer, wispy dress came to mid-thigh, plummeted in the front to reveal well-rounded cleavage, and was held together by lacy spaghetti straps at the shoulders.

She was provocative in her walk, sensual without trying to be. As she neared his standing position, brushing past him to make use of the three-way mirror beside him, she accidentally bumped into him, not having realized he stood there.

"Oh, I'm so sorry."

Smoky. Her voice reminded him of billowing, velvet smoke. Or silk sheets and sweaty sex. He coughed discreetly into his hand. "It's no trouble." He smiled, looking down into her light green eyes. A dusting of freckles across the bridge of her nose should have made her less appealing but only served to heighten her exotic look. "I should have known better than to stand in front of the only three-way mirror nearest the women's changing room."

He had made the omission in all seriousness, but she smiled warmly up to him and laughed. He found himself grinning back, pleased he'd inadvertently delighted her.

"Poor guy. You're liable to get stampeded around here."

She had a sultry southern American accent that worked its way down his spine. "I shall endeavor not to come to a bad end."

She laughed again. He averted his gaze and discretely coughed into his hand. The woman held the most primitive fascination for him.

"Well, good luck then."

She glided away from him and stood in front of the mirror, taking in how the dress looked at all angles. He could have told her how it looked had she asked him. Sinfully riveting.

When she stood before the mirror to look at herself from the front, Neil was able to see without any trouble whatsoever that she was wearing white bikini-thong panties beneath the dress. Her buttocks molded around the scant piece of material as if made for it, two globes of no doubt tanned flesh partitioned off with a piece of lacy white cloth.

He quickly looked away, pushing his gold-wired spectacles up the bridge of his nose as he did so. He blew out a breath, his penis erect.

A saleswoman thankfully interrupted the lecherous direction his thoughts were headed in, smiling brightly as she made her way towards the American woman. He took another deep breath and expelled it. He wished Margaret would hurry.

"You look absolutely divine!" the saleswoman said with a bit too much enthusiasm, the way people working for commissions are apt to do. This saleswoman, however, wasn't lying. The emerald-eyed American with the full lips and ripe breasts did look divine. He idly wondered how much of it was the dress and how much was simply the woman herself.

"You think so?" She scrunched up her nose and glanced back into the mirror. "I was thinking it looked okay, but I wasn't sure."

"Perfect!" the redheaded saleswoman gushed. "Much better than the last one. Absolutely breathtaking."

The American smiled slowly, as if she understood what the clerk was about. The petite redhead wanted a sale. "Great. I'll take it then."

Ten minutes later, Margaret emerged from the dressing room, having settled on a sensible pair of brown camel tweed trousers remarkably similar to the first pair she'd tried on. He smiled down to her before they made their way to the cash register where even now the American and the redheaded sales clerk were chatting back and forth about everything and nothing. The redhead was extremely pert for the American was spending a great deal of money. "You will look absolutely ravishing at the Ballast party in this dress."

The American merely smiled. "Thanks." She handed her a Visa card. "By the way, when does the festival begin? I was under the impression it lasted the entire month of August but apparently not."

"Next week," the redhead answered as she accepted the Visa into her palm. "It lasts three weeks, not four," she said in the way of explanation.

Her customer sighed. "I wonder what I'll do with myself until then. Maybe I'll drive up to the Highlands," she said rather wistfully. "I've never seen them before."

"Excellent notion." The redhead scanned the credit card, practically salivating when it came back with an acceptance. "There's a terrific beach resort in Strathy Point that attracts a lot of tourism." She leaned in closer to the

American and whispered confidentially as she handed her the receipt to be signed. "I've heard it told they allow you to strut about topless up there in the summer months." She winked. "Sounds like a great diversion to me."

Neil could feel Margaret stiffen up beside him. Clearly, the redhead had unwittingly offended her sense of propriety.

"You're right," the American said without pretense, "it sounds fun. What's the name of the place again?"

"Strathy Point."

She nodded. "Guess I know where I'm headed for a few days. Thanks for the heads-up."

The redhead waved that away as she took back the receipt. "Think nothing—oh my!"

The American's golden brown head shot up. She regarded the saleswoman quizzically.

"You're Valentina Jason-Elliot? The woman who writes those sexy suspense thrillers?"

Neil's ears perked up. He'd read a couple of her novels himself.

"One and the same."

"I love your work! When is the next one due out?"

The American's face colored slightly. An effect Neil found oddly charming. "At the end of the month."

"Excellent!"

A minute and an autograph later, the golden brown American with the blood-red nails made her way out of Jenners, shopping bags in tow. Neil watched her walk away, out of his life forever, and wished he'd had no reaction to that knowledge one way or the other.

* * * * *

"Neil," Margaret said hesitantly, "we must talk."

Following her into her mum's formal living room, he inclined his head. "By all means." He took the seat she indicated, wondering what this could possibly be about.

Margaret took her time getting to the heart of the matter, picking a piece of imaginary lint from her new trousers as she gathered up her courage. Neil eyed her curiously, uncertain as to what was going on. "Margaret?" he gently prodded.

She looked up, ever the nervous mouse. "Neil, I'm sorry to say this, but I..." Her voice trailed off as she looked away.

"What? What is it?"

Her cheeks pinkened as she regarded him. "I'm afraid this isn't working out for me," she whispered.

He stilled, his entire body unmoving for a long moment. "I beg your pardon?" His eyebrows drew together. "I thought we were getting on admirably well."

"Oh we are," she rushed out, her mousy brown head shooting upward. "It's just that...that..."

"Yes?"

She sighed. "Neil, let me come straight to the point."

He nodded.

"What are your intentions?" She went back to picking the invisible lint from her trousers. Her cheeks scalded from pink to crimson. "Do you plan to marry me?"

"Margaret, I—"

"I'm sorry!" she blithered out. "But Neil, I'm to turn thirty-two next week. My biological clock is ticking quite madly." She briefly closed her eyes, embarrassed. "So I need to know your intentions," she squeaked.

In that moment he knew he couldn't marry her, inducing a certain sadness to settle in. He'd been hesitant all along, not wanting to deal with his feelings on the issue. But now, having been backed into a proverbial corner by Margaret, he realized with crystal clarity that they would not deal well together for a lifetime.

Neil genuinely liked her and respected her, but the differences between them were vast. She was too churchy, too timid. He was too authoritative, too brusque—or in comparison at any rate. But she was a good woman, and a woman who deserved to be given the truth.

Neil sighed, his mood glum. Damn it, he truly did care for Margaret. The last thing in the world he wanted was to hurt her. He reached for her hand and took it in his own. "You are all things worthy and wonderful," he said gently, "but I..." He took a deep breath and prepared to give her the truth she sought. "But I don't think a marriage between us would work," he softly finished.

Margaret nodded, but said nothing.

"I'm terribly sorry. Perhaps if we took things a wee bit slower, gave our relationship a little more time—"

She held up a palm. "I've already wasted two and a half months of my life on you, Dr. Macalister." She was angrier than he'd ever seen her before. "I think it best if you just leave."

Neil hesitated for a brief moment before relenting. He stood up, looking down on her. "I wish you well, Margaret."

She closed her eyes. "Please just leave."

He inclined his head, feeling lecherous for the second time in the same afternoon, though for differing reasons. Hurting a woman he genuinely cared for had not been in today's, or any day's, plan. When she gave him her back, Neil left without further ado, not wanting to cause her any more grief than was necessary.

By the time he reached his car, he felt older and more tired than he could ever recall feeling. He frowned as he tightly grasped onto the steering wheel.

It occurred to Neil that the mousy, churchy Margaret had just worked up the nerve to dump him.

He grunted. So much for her alleged timidity.

Chapter 2

Churchy, timid Margaret had dumped him. If that didn't beat all, he doubted anything would.

Neil sighed at yesterday's memory as he made his way into the University of Edinburgh and towards his office. He needed to prepare lecture notes, as classes were due to commence in a fortnight. Taking a seat behind his desk, he steepled his fingertips together and considered the state of his life.

He frowned. *Dull* was the only word he could think of to describe it.

Neil had never been the type of man others thought of as particularly exciting. He'd known this fact all of his life, but until this moment the knowledge of it hadn't exactly bothered him.

Growing up, he'd been a sickly but hardworking child who excelled in his studies and harbored a deep love of mathematics. A skinny, gawky lad, he'd reveled in the identity his school grades had given him, realizing it was the one thing he was better at than most. Firmly entrenched in the identity of nerd by the time he was thirteen, he had even begun to dress the part.

He hadn't gone ballistic, he reminded himself, for he'd always been a fine dresser. But he'd donned spectacles instead of purchasing contact lenses and had dressed in his formal lecturer's attire from an indecently young age.

And now at the age of thirty-nine, there was no way of living down his geeky claim to fame. That he had grown out of his sickliness and had acquired an athletic, muscled body was of no import. People saw what they wanted to see, what they expected to see, and from the age of thirteen onward it had been expected that Neil Macalister was a nerd.

But had he done anything to expel such a notion? No, he thought grimly, he hadn't. He'd been content in his role as the boring and reliable lecturer of mathematics, content with allowing the status quo to remain...

Until he'd met *her*.

Neil's eyes flicked towards the bookshelf standing on the opposite side of his office. Withdrawing slowly from his seat, he made his way past the sofa he sometimes slept on when working late into the night and over to the oak structure, stopping to pick up a copy of *The Scream*. It was the latest release of one Valentina Jason-Elliot.

Now that he'd been well and truly dumped by Margaret, he was able to mentally confess something to himself he hadn't been able to admit to before. Namely that when a certain author had run into him yesterday, all green eyes and red smiles, he had wanted so much for her to see him as more than a boring lecturer of mathematics, as more than a sensible man in proper clothing.

He had wanted her to see him as a virile male who had picked up her scent and was onto it.

He snorted at his ridiculous musings. As if that were possible.

And yet Neil found himself wondering, not for the first time, just what *had* gone through the novelist's mind whilst conversing with him. What had she thought of him? Or had she thought anything of him at all? Probably not.

Neil sighed, placing *The Scream* on the shelf it had been occupying. He made his way back to his desk and plopped rather unceremoniously down into his seat. Running his fingers briskly through his short, dark hair he attempted to squelch the restlessness brewing inside of him, telling himself it did no good whatsoever to obsess over a woman who didn't so much as know his name and most likely wouldn't care to learn it.

Even now as he sat at his sensible desk surrounded by sensible items from a sensible lecturer's life, he couldn't help but to consider Ms. Jason-Elliot's current insensible whereabouts. He knew precisely where she was, exactly what she was doing, for he would have had to been deaf to have not overheard the conversation she'd engaged in yesterday with the redheaded saleswoman.

The object of his desire was at Strathy Point. Possibly lying topless on the beach somewhere this very moment. The mental image alone caused him to become painfully erect.

Absently rubbing his palm alongside the outline of his jaw, Neil asked himself if he had the nerve to use this insider knowledge and do something completely out of character...something impulsive like follow Valentina Jason-Elliot to Strathy Point and attempt to become reacquainted with her.

A very intoxicating, yet highly unnerving prospect.

What if, after all, she had no desire to so much as speak to him? What if he made a fool of himself?

Neil was about to discard the notion entirely when the image of churchy, timid Margaret dumping him popped into his mind. He frowned. If the mouse could find the nerve to cut her losses after a mere two months of dating, then surely he could find the nerve to pay a visit to Strathy Point.

Indeed, Neil thought as he surged to his feet, sick to death of his boring life, tired of the status quo, why the bloody hell not?

* * * * *

The salesclerk had been both right and wrong. It was a topless beach, yes, but it was a bottomless beach, too. Valentina shrugged the knowledge off as she ignored the aroused looks a few of the male tourists were throwing her way. Her parents had been taking her to nude beaches since she'd been old enough to walk so she truly didn't find anything all that remarkable about seeing naked bodies scattered around.

Still, she wasn't naïve enough to believe that everyone saw life the way she did. Most of the men were here simply because they wanted to stare.

Valentina found an area to herself a bit off from the other beachgoers. Spreading out a blanket on the sandy shore, she wound her hair into a topknot and plopped down onto the blanket. Rummaging through her beach bag, she located a bottle of tanning accelerator and began working it into her shoulders and breasts. The chilly liquid caused her nipples to harden, elongated buttons of rosy flesh poking up from the puffy areolas that surrounded them.

After she'd finished coating her arms and legs, she laid back on the blanket, her hands supporting the weight of her head. Her nipples poked further upward, their reaction to the sun causing a slight carnal aching to knot in her belly.

Valentina closed her eyes, her mind wandering as her face and body grew a rich golden brown from the sun's rays. As her thoughts strayed, she found them meandering two days backward in time to that attractive-looking man she'd met at Jenners.

The weird thing about it was, the guy really wasn't her type. And Valentina was well aware of what her type was. Why she had given so much as a passing thought to the studious, conservative-looking man, she couldn't say.

She was used to dating musicians and artists, the sort of men that had a certain reckless air about them, the sort of men who were forever jaunting off to try this new thing or that due to the sheer restlessness of their natures. Of course, Valentina admitted to herself, it was that very restlessness that had caused her last boyfriend to stray from her in the first place, taking on new lovers without even so much as a passing concern of what it might do to her heart.

If there was one thing that man back in Jenners could not be called, it was restless. Valentina smiled, thinking that the stranger had waited on whomever he'd escorted to the department store with an unnatural amount of male patience. If that had been her ex-boyfriend, Allen, he would have been trying to get up the redheaded saleswoman's skirt as a way to pass the time while waiting on his girlfriend or wife to emerge from the changing room.

Valentina's mind wandered a bit further, wondering to herself as she was if a lack of restlessness in a man was necessarily a bad thing. She considered the patient stranger, not at all the type who looked like he came on to just anything in a skirt. She idly wondered if he was patient in all areas of his life, namely in bed, then told herself she was acting like an idiot for even contemplating it.

The proper-looking stranger was in Edinburgh, which might as well be an ocean away since she had no idea who he was or how to find him should she feel inclined to try. Besides, she reminded herself, he could be married for all she knew, and one thing she would never consider doing was dallying with a married or otherwise attached man.

Valentina fell asleep in the sun a minute later, her last coherent thought revolving around whether or not the stranger had noticed her as a woman.

And why in the world she should care.

Chapter 3

Neil slowly walked along the beach at Strathy Point feeling a bit surreal. He couldn't believe he'd actually entertained a notion like trotting off to the Highlands in the hopes of espying the American novelist, let alone seeing it through. But he was here now, he told himself resolutely, so he might as well make the most of it.

The beach was a nude one, he noted. He felt a bit awkward in that he'd retained his swimming trunks whilst everyone around him was completely divested of clothing. This beach wasn't a topless one as the sales clerk had suggested, but both a topless and bottomless one. He felt like an idiot.

Neil batted his eyelashes a few times in rapid succession, the contacts he'd procured yesterday afternoon making his eyes water a bit. He was growing used to the damned things—for the most part—but conceded it had taken a few painful hours to get even this far. Well, he thought with a measure of satisfaction, should he be lucky enough to run into Valentina Jason-Elliot at least he wouldn't be doing it in his sensible, boring spectacles.

Neil scanned the shoreline of the beach for the woman in question, his gut knotting in anticipation of seeing her again. His dark gaze flicked this way and that until at last it settled upon the form of a sleeping and very nude author lying a ways off down the sandy terrain.

He took a deep breath to steady himself, praying to heaven that he'd find the courage to approach her and awaken her. He could only hope his body cooperated and that he didn't sustain a noticeably large and painful erection at the merest glimpse of her. But when he drew closer and saw that her large rosy nipples were poking up into the air, his desire to fall down beside her and suck on them sent all thoughts of retaining his control scurrying away.

He sighed, noting with grim resignation that his penis was as hard as a tire iron.

He went down on his knees beside her, unable to believe that he, Neil Macalister, had grown bold enough to approach her let alone be brazen enough to drop to his knees and ogle her body up close. He glanced around quickly, feeling a moment's panic at being embarrassed in front of others should she shout at him to go away. He breathed in relief when he realized they were quite alone on this stretch of beach and her shouts would only serve to humiliate him in front of her. Not that that prospect was much better.

Neil's eyes fell to her face, noting at once that she was in a deep sleep. Reckless, that. He had the urge to scold her for it, then frowned at his thoughts.

He sighed. He couldn't be more the geek if he tried, he thought grimly. Here he was, sitting before the object of his obsession, her body completely naked to his perusal, and his thoughts had turned to scolding her?

Still, he couldn't help but consider that if he'd been any man but himself he might have taken advantage of the situation and forced himself on her. She should be more careful.

His dark eyes found her breasts and all thoughts of scolding a certain novelist flew out the proverbial window. His penis stiffened as he regarded her, desire coming fast and hard. Her areolas, he noticed, were a light pink and a tad puffy. Her elongated rouge nipples shot up out of them like two bottle rockets on velvety soft launching pads.

Neil took a deep breath, his erection fierce, as his gaze meandered lower and settled upon her puffed up labia. One of her knees was bent slightly, offering his vision no impediment to finding out what her flesh looked like on the inside. She kept her mons shaved bald, he noted as his jaw tightened, thinking to himself how much he'd love to run his tongue all about the sleek folds beneath it.

Neil stared at her cunt, wanting to suck on it, wanting to ride in it, wanting it period. As if the sleeping woman could read his thoughts and wanted to encourage them, the flesh between her thighs grew a bit wet before his eyes, one pearly drop of fluid noticeable at the entrance.

His eyes shot up to her breasts. They were harder then before. So hard it looked painful to him. So hard he envisioned taking them into his mouth and —

Realization dawned.

Embarrassed at having been caught looking his fill at her naked body, Neil's gaze shot up and clashed with a very awake woman's. He coughed into his hand as she smiled at him, and like that geeky boy he'd been at thirteen, he had the sudden urge to bolt.

Her eyebrows softly drew together as she looked at him curiously. "Haven't we met?" she asked on a smile.

* * * * *

Valentina thought she had grown too jaded to become aroused by something as simple as a man gazing at her naked body with desire. But Christ, she thought as her nipples stabbed up into the air, this man's brooding gaze had an unnerving effect on her.

He looked at her like he wanted to own her, like he wanted to shove his fingers up her cunt and claim it. The effect was a heady one, an arousing one, and it wasn't just because she was being ogled in general but because she'd already realized whom she was being ogled by.

Mr. Prim and Proper himself. The stranger she'd chatted briefly with at Jenners.

Valentina's eyes ran over the length of him. He was impressively built, she thought. His legs were long and well-muscled, his arms not overly big like a body-builder's, but alluringly cut and vein-roped. His chest was equally well-muscled, hard and tempting. And his cock — good God — she smiled, thinking herself to be definitely *not* jaded, his cock was gloriously long and thick, bulging against his swimming trunks.

Knowing that the sight of her was turning him on, that this man she'd fallen asleep thinking about was here beside her, caused her belly to clench and liquid drops to form between her thighs. His gaze shot up, snagging hers, and his face turned charmingly red as he coughed into his hand.

She could tell he meant to leave. Alarmed at the prospect, and not having the time or inclination to ponder why, she forestalled him with a smile and a simple question. "Haven't we met?"

* * * * *

Neil's eyes flicked towards her nipples then back to her face. He nervously cleared his throat, feeling like the biggest idiot to have ever walked the planet. "Y-Yes," he stammered out, nodding once, "we met at Jenners two days back."

She smiled at his rich brogue, coming up on her elbows then settling back on them while they chatted. Her nipples were scant inches away from his face, all hard and tempting, resting on their puffy pink patches. She made no move to close her thighs, he realized, and had in fact opened one leg a bit wider. She was not shy at all over having been caught completely nude. She seemed to revel in this intimate moment between them, and he wasn't altogether certain what to make of that fact.

"I knew I recognized you." She grinned, settling him down a bit when he understood that she wasn't angry at his ogling. "Did you ever end up getting stampeded?"

"Stampeded?" he asked dumbly. And then, remembering their earlier conversation, he smiled. "No. I made it out of the store in one piece."

"Good." Valentina bit down onto her lip and gnawed at it a moment, unable to believe she was about to suggest what she was. But she felt brazen. Aroused and brazen. And she knew that she wanted to have sex with this man. She'd never been one to think beyond the present and in this moment in time she wanted him. "You know," she said as she tilted her chin, "this situation seems a bit unfair to me."

Neil's face colored. "How so?"

She glanced at his tented swimming trunks. "This is a nude beach," she murmured, "but you're wearing clothes."

Neil's cock grew harder, the muscles in his stomach clenching. She had basically just invited him to remove all of his clothing, even knowing as she had to that he was fully erect. He glanced down at her labia which was now ripe and swollen and wondered if it was possible that she actually wanted to have sex with him.

He doubted it, but decided for once in his life to just go with the flow and see what happened. He stood up and lowered the swim trunks, his erection now fully revealed to her.

Valentina's breath caught, not having expected him to be *that* well-endowed. He was handsome in a very harsh, masculine way, and sexy in a very naughty-schoolgirl-corrupts-the-handsome-distinguished-professor kind of way. She smiled at him as he resumed his seat beside her. "The sun feels great against the skin, doesn't it?" she drawled.

"Quite." As Neil gazed at her nipples, he decided that his tendency to lecture found odd moments to make itself known. "Though I hope you've some manner of protection on," he added, "for you wouldn't want to burn your—" He coughed discreetly into his hand and looked away, embarrassed at what he'd almost uttered.

Valentina was enjoying this. Most of the men she'd dated had been too sure of themselves, as if they believed they had the right to take what they wanted. But this man was so arousingly unique that she found herself wanting to push him more and more, if for no other reason than to test his limits of endurance. "Why don't you rub some lotion into them for me?" she whispered.

His dark eyes shot up to meet hers and he visibly gulped. He didn't throw himself at her, but neither did he back down from her carnal challenge. "Where is the lotion?" he rasped out.

He was hard, so goddamned hard.

"In my bag."

A few moments later, Neil had worked the coconut-scented lotion into his palms and was reaching for her breasts. He drew them into his large hands, moistening the soft fleshy globes with the sweet oil. When her breathing grew a bit shallow, he began massaging her nipples, working the lotion into them with his thumbs and fingers.

"What's your name?" Valentina asked breathlessly, her eyes flickering shut as he continued the sensual massage.

"Neil Macalister," he answered thickly, his arousal causing his inhibitions to wane significantly. "And you are Valentina Jason-Elliot."

Her eyes flew open. "How did you know my name?"

"I overheard the saleswoman."

She stilled. "Did you also overhear me tell her I'd be vacationing at Strathy Point?"

His dark gaze clashed with her light green one. "Yes," he admitted, offering no further explanation.

He massaged her nipples a bit harder, plucking at them now. When she moaned softly and her eyes narrowed in desire, he feared for spilling himself right there on her thigh.

"You followed me." It was a statement not a question.

"Yes." It was the truth not an apology.

"I'm not sure what to think of that."

"I think," Neil said softly, his erection achingly swollen, "that your beautiful cunt needs lotioned up as well." He stilled as soon as the words came tumbling out, not quite believing he'd actually spoken them.

Valentina met his gaze and studied his features, as if considering his words. And then, surreal as it was to him, she splayed her legs wide, granting him not only a delicious view of her bald cunt and its silky folds, but permission to massage her in the most intimate manner possible.

Neil forgot all about the lotion as his index finger found her hole and he pushed a large finger up inside of her. She exhaled on a moan, her head falling back to dangle precariously from her neck, as her wet pussy grew wetter and her nipples continued to stab upwards.

A second finger found her pussy hole, joining with the first, as he slowly began to finger-fuck it. On his other hand the pad of his thumb zeroed in on her clit and he began to rub it in a sensual, circular motion. She arched into his hand, breathing deeply as he massaged her soaked flesh.

"You have the most beautiful cunt I've ever seen," he said hoarsely, "so wet and juicy, so tight and swollen."

"Oh yess*s*." Valentina's back arched further, her lips parting slightly. She was drunk on arousal, intoxicated by his effect on her.

His words, his hands, his mere presence heightened her desire. Neil made her feel like an omnipotent erotic goddess — a sensual state of being no other man had worked her into. He looked at her as if she was the most intriguing woman in the world, explored her body as though he'd never get enough of it.

"Come for me, Tina," she heard him murmur. His fingers began to thrust faster. The rubbing motion on her clit became brisker. "I want to watch you come."

Oh yes — oh God she was coming. She was so close. She groaned, her hips rearing up for him, wanting him to do what he would, wanting to come hard for him.

His fingers were pushing up inside of her, filling her wet flesh, stretching her and making her ache for his cock. The sun was beating down on her, the wind was chilling her nipples, further tightening them.

His face dove for her pussy as he finger-fucked her. She gasped as his tongue curled around her clit, replacing the pad of his thumb. She thought she'd died and gone to a sinner's heaven. "*Neil.*"

He lapped at her quickly, flicking his tongue across the swollen bud, slurping it up into his mouth and sucking mercilessly. Valentina's entire body began to shake as he sucked on her and sucked on her, never relenting, never even slowing. "*Oh God — oh yes, Neil.*"

The low guttural sound of appreciation he made in the back of his throat was her undoing. Instinctually, she reached out for his head, threaded her crimson nails through his dark hair, and pressed his face into her cunt as far as it would go. He sucked harder still, slurping sounds reaching her ears.

"*Yes.*"

Valentina's hips reared upwards as a devastating orgasm ripped through her belly. She screamed at the intensity of it, her entire body spasming, her flesh convulsing around his fingers.

And then he was coming down on top of her, crushing her into the blanket as he settled himself between her thighs. Their gazes clashed as his hands palmed her breasts and with one powerful thrust he surged inside of her.

"*Neil.*"

"Christ you feel good," he gritted out, thrusting into her faster and faster. He wanted to go slow, to savor this moment in time he doubted he'd get a repeat performance of. But her flesh was so hot and it kept suctioning him back in, taking him deeper, making the need to brand her insides with his hot cum paramount. He groaned, his eyelids heavy with arousal.

Valentina moaned, wrapping her legs around Neil's waist. He plucked at her nipples in response, clamping down on them as he surged inside of her over and over, deeper and deeper, again and again. The sound of flesh slapping flash filled his ears, further ignited his desire.

"Fuck me harder," she gasped, grinding her hips at him.

Neil's jaw clenched as he gave her what she wanted. He released her breasts, slid his hands beneath their joined bodies to palm her buttocks, and pounded into her wet flesh in a series of deep, merciless thrusts.

"*Oh God.*"

Valentina closed her eyes and held on for a hard ride, her legs wrapped firmly about his middle, giving him the ability to deeply penetrate her. She could hear the sounds of her flesh sucking his cock inside of her body each time he buried himself to the hilt.

And then she was coming, spasming around his cock, her back arching as he repeatedly sank into her. She screamed out her release, wrapping her legs tighter about his waist, bringing pressure down on her clit, which made her scream all the louder. "*OH — GOD!*"

"*Jesus.*" Neil thrust into her cunt — deep, hard — oblivious to anything but the feel of her flesh wrapped around him. He sank into her again and again, gluttonously indulging himself of her body. He felt like an animal — territorial, primal, unable to entertain a coherent thought. All he could do was feel — feel this woman, feel this cunt he was obsessed with possessing and fucking. "*Tina.*"

And then he was pouring himself into her, hot cum spurting into the body of the woman he wanted to brand, the pussy he'd wanted to fuck and had never thought he stood a chance of plunging into. His muscles bunched, his entire body clenched, as he closed his eyes and pumped enough cum inside of her to put three men to shame.

His breathing harsh, Neil gazed down into Valentina's face as he hovered over her. She was smiling dreamily, the way a woman who'd been fucked hard and good was apt to do, and in that moment he felt more possessive of her sweet cunt than he had a right to.

He fell down on top of her, replete and exhausted, the most ferocious orgasm of his life rendering him all but unconscious. He found enough strength to tip his head and sip from her lips before rolling off of her and hoisting his body up beside hers.

Anyone could walk down the beach and find them here, he knew. But he was tired, so incredibly tired.

Neil's dark head came down to rest on Valentina's breasts, his heavy eyelids closing. As he fell into a smoky slumber it occurred to him from somewhere in the haze of his semi-unconsciousness that she might try to leave him, might be gone when he woke up.

Instinctually, inevitably, Neil's hand found her engorged flesh. He thrust two fingers deep inside of her cunt, locking them together, and fell fast asleep.

Chapter 4

Neil awoke to the feel of his achingly erect shaft disappearing into the depths of Valentina's throat. Her full lips devoured the length of him, then resurfaced to tease the extremely sensitive head. He groaned, grabbing her by her golden brown hair. His jaw clenched as she made an appreciative "Mmmm" sound and her lips glided up and down his shaft.

She licked the length of him like a lollipop, closed her eyes and sucked on him like it was a favorite treat. "Mmm mmm mmmmmm."

"*Christ.*" Neil gritted his teeth, unable to endure another moment. On a hoarse groan he climaxed into her mouth.

He shuddered all over again as he watched her lips and tongue lap up all of his juice, then suck on the tiny hole of his sensitive head to make certain she'd missed nothing. He gasped, his eyes closing as his chest heaved up and down.

When his breathing steadied and he was able to open his eyes again, the first thing he noticed was that the sun had sunk below the horizon and evening had descended. The second thing he noticed, and the better of the two, was that a beautiful bald cunt was lowering itself onto his mouth.

Valentina's blood-red nails spread her pussy lips far apart, which served to make her tiny rosebud clit bulge out further. "Suck on me, Neil," she murmured in that smoky Southern American drawl, "I love the way you eat pussy."

There was no time for a reply, for her wet cunt had found his lips and his tongue was shooting out to flick at her clit and curl around it. He drew the sensitive piece of flesh into his mouth and began to suckle from it in long, drugging sips.

"Neil."

Valentina began to ride his face in slow undulations, the same as she would have ridden his cock. Her head fell back, her unbound hair cascading onto his stomach, as she moaned into the night and rode him. Each time her hips lurched back in their circular motion her clit was tugged at by Neil's lips and suctioning tongue. She moaned, her nipples stabbing out as her orgasm drew nearer.

Neil groaned appreciatively, his hands reaching up to cup and knead her buttocks. Valentina began riding his mouth faster as he massaged the twin globes, her drenched flesh pressing into his warm mouth.

"God yes."

Neil began to suckle hard from her clit, drawing from her relentlessly, forcing her to gasp and moan, to undulate on top of him in frenzied arousal. He could feel her body shake and stiffen simultaneously, letting him know that she was coming. He sucked harder, offering her no mercy, wanting her to think of him and him alone when she needed release.

"Neil."

Valentina expelled his name on a primitive moan, her hips thrashing madly, her cunt drenching his face with its dew. Her nipples stiffened into impossibly tight points as her flesh convulsed around his mouth and blood rushed up to heat her face.

Panting heavily, Valentina ground her throbbing vagina one last time into Neil's mouth, then slid it down his lips, down his chin, gliding down toward his chest. He thrust his tongue out, lapping at her in one long lick from her hole to her clit as her soaked flesh slid off his face.

"*Mmmm.*" Valentina smiled down to him as she perched herself on his chest. "That was great."

Neil's eyes flicked toward the distended nipples that hovered over his line of vision. He reached up and cupped her breasts, plucking at her nipples in a way he knew she liked. "I've got something else I want you to ride," he murmured.

Valentina grinned, knowing his erect manhood was poking at her, wanting entrance. "I'll have to think about it," she teased.

But Neil was in no mood to be teased. He felt like an animal in heat, a beast that wanted to rut inside of its mate. "Sit on my cock," he said demandingly, no trace of humor in his voice.

Valentina was surprised at the way her body responded to his dominant tone, soaking itself for a smooth entry, submissively preparing itself to be fucked. She grabbed him by the base of the penis, drew herself up to her knees, and sank down onto his stiff shaft, impaling herself in one fluid motion. "Better?" she breathed out.

"Infinitely."

Neil plucked at the puffy nipples he loved so much as she rode him long and hard. For the next twenty minutes he glutted on her flesh, greedily accepting all of her climaxes, all of her moans.

He was obsessed with her, he knew. Obsessed with her body, obsessed with her cunt, wanting to own it. He was obsessed with her, period.

As his muscles bunched and corded and he spurted his hot cum deep inside of her body, he also realized something else. When they were alone like this, together like this, mating like two animals in full rut, he was more in touch with who he was as a man than he'd ever been before.

There was no need to hide behind proper façades where Valentina Jason-Elliot was concerned. No roles, no assumed identities.

There was just Neil Macalister.

Chapter 5

"So tell me about yourself. After the night we just spent together on the beach I'd love to have my curiosity indulged a bit." Valentina grinned at Neil as she sat across from him in the hotel's tiny restaurant. They were dressed casually today, both of them wearing simple jeans and tee-shirt combos; an everyday event for Valentina, an anomaly for Neil.

Neil grinned back, feeling more carefree than he could ever remember being. The fact that he didn't feel the need to conform to a predetermined role was manifested in everything from his casual attire to the fact that he'd just spent the last several hours making love on a nude beach to a gloriously sexual woman ten years his junior. He felt wonderful, alive and wonderful. He never wanted their interlude to end.

"I'm a lecturer of mathematics at the University of Edinburgh," he said as he picked up his glass of Cabernet Sauvignon. "I've been there for close to eighteen years now."

Valentina smiled, his deep brogue sending warm, fuzzy feelings down her spine. "Have you ever been married?"

"No."

"Ever come close?"

"Once." He shrugged, the memory of his college sweetheart feeling like a lifetime ago. "But in the end Susan decided a lecturer of physics was more her style."

Valentina knowingly nodded. "So she was having an affair. My last relationship came to an end for that reason, too."

"Someone cheated on *you*?"

Neil had asked the question incredulously, as if he couldn't fathom any man so much as even considering sleeping around when he had Valentina to come home to. The fact that he felt that way to begin with sent butterflies coursing through her belly and made an unidentifiable emotion lodge in her heart.

He thought she was perfect. Apparently he thought every man on the planet should feel the same way. She didn't agree, knew she was far from perfect, but such feelings on his part made her want him all the more.

"Yeah, he did." She smiled wryly. "Multiple times actually."

Neil reached out and touched her hand. "Are you okay now?"

Her answer was important to him for a couple of reasons, he knew. He didn't want her hurting and just as importantly he didn't want her pining away for another man. Such a thought, he possessively admitted, was far from pleasant.

"Yeah I'm fine." She grinned, her eyes crinkling at the corners. "At the time I was pretty upset. For three days I meandered around the house feeling dramatically tragic. But when the fourth day came and I no longer cared I realized that I couldn't have been in love."

His eyebrows rose slightly. "How so?"

She splayed her hands in a gesture that Neil took to mean he should have already known the answer. "I was over Allen in three days. If I'd been in love with him it seems to me I'd have walked around feeling tragic for at least another couple of weeks." She chuckled. "Or at least another couple of days."

Neil smiled, more elated by the knowledge that she hadn't loved Allen than he should have been, than he had a right to be. He had no idea, after all, if Valentina planned to continue their affair beyond Strathy Point. Because such a topic didn't settle well with him he discarded it, refusing to deal with anything other than the here and now. And right now he was here with her. It was all that mattered.

"So," Valentina cheerily interjected, breaking him from his thoughts, "how long do you plan to vacation up here?"

Neil smiled wryly. "How long do you plan to stay?"

She laughed, remembering his earlier confession that he'd followed her to the beach. She supposed such an event should have frightened her somewhat, but it didn't. Perhaps if there was something weird about him, or if the attraction wasn't mutual, she would have been alarmed.

But she most definitely was not alarmed. On the contrary, it made her feel terrifically sexy that Neil would go to such lengths to be with her.

"I'll be here another three days. Well, not here exactly, but in the Highlands in general." She shrugged. "I planned on leaving Strathy Point this afternoon and going camping on Cairn Gorm for a couple of days."

"Camping sounds lovely," he unthinkingly murmured, their gazes locking.

Reality dawned for a fraction of a moment and his face slightly colored as he broke eye contact. He'd just all but invited himself along when she was most likely ready to be rid of him.

"I meant to say that I'm certain you will have an excell—"

"You wanna come?"

His dark head shot up. He swallowed hard. "You want me to join you?" he asked tentatively, thinking he must have misunderstood her intentions.

"Definitely." She grinned. "The question is do *you* want to join *me*?"

He blew out a breath. "If you don't mind," he murmured, deciding not to question his good luck.

"I don't mind." Valentina shook her head and smiled. "I don't mind at all."

* * * * *

"It's beautiful up here."

"Indeed. It truly is."

Valentina glanced curiously up at Neil while they worked together to pitch the tent. Between checking out and returning her rental car, they had gotten a late start leaving Strathy Point so it was already close to midnight. Luckily it wasn't totally dark outside for the sun never truly sets in the Highlands during the summer.

"You said that almost nostalgically," she murmured.

Neil shrugged, but the gesture was far from casual. "It's a shame, I'm well aware, but I've lived just a few hours drive away from here all of my life and never took the time to experience it for myself."

"Cairn Gorm you mean? The mountain we're on?"

"Yes." He smiled, gazing down at her, his dark eyes raking over her clothed breasts, sweeping across her shielded mons before returning to study the tent they'd just pitched together. "That and other things."

Valentina's body had an immediate reaction to his casual perusal and carnal insinuations. Her nipples tightened into elongated pink buds and a liquid heat infused her belly. She observed him through hooded eyes, very much turned on, very much wanting him.

She shook it off, telling herself this was no time to be concerned with her libido. They had pitched the tent, true, but it still needed some fixing up on the inside. Besides, it was quite chilly out and they also needed to start a fire.

"Tell me about yourself," Neil said as he began arranging kindling within the pile of logs. "Between our conversation in the restaurant this morning and our drive up to the mountains tonight I doubt if there's anything left to tell about me. You, however, are still an enigma."

"An enigma?" Valentina glanced over her shoulder, momentarily distracted from her work of smoothing out the bottom of the tent. "I'd hardly call myself that." She smiled, resuming her work. "What would you like to know?"

Everything, Neil thought. "Whatever you'd like to tell." He located a box of matches and struck one against its grainy side, igniting it. "I gathered from your accent that you're from somewhere in the southern United States, but I can't quite pinpoint where."

"Georgia," she replied somewhat muffled, her face inside of the tent while she arranged things as she wanted them. "Atlanta."

"Ah." Neil smiled, absently noting that the kindling was now lit and the log settled on top of it was starting to go ablaze. He glanced over his shoulder. "A Georgia peach. I—"

He stopped mid-sentence, distracted by the sight of her lush derriere pointing skywards. She was down on all fours, the upper half of her body buried inside of the tent doing who knew what, the lower half of her jeans-clad body bared to the elements.

In a sensual daze he stood up, taking to his feet as he walked up behind her. He ran his hand over her buttocks, causing her to gasp as he slipped his fingers in between her thighs and rubbed her clit through the denim. "Take your clothes off," he said brusquely. "Now."

It occurred to Neil from somewhere in the back of his aroused mind that his voice had sounded a bit harsh even to himself. But he couldn't seem to stop himself, couldn't seem to tamper down his commands.

When he was near her like this and his thoughts turned carnal, he felt no more intellectually advanced than a Neanderthal, a caveman that wanted to rut inside of the mate he'd claimed. He'd never been like this before with any other woman and because of that fact he didn't know how to control it. Nor was he certain that he cared to.

Valentina came up on her knees, turning around to regard him. Her light green eyes had gone wide, clearly having been surprised by the tone of his voice. But he offered no rebuttals, no apologies.

"Take your clothes off," he repeated without so much as a flinch, his dark eyes narrowed in desire. "You may finish your work after you've removed them."

Valentina's nipples hardened instantaneously. She should have been outraged by his words, or at least offended by them, but she wasn't. She liked playing the submissive to him on a sexual level, reveled in the way he dominated her body as though he owned it.

Neil Macalister was an egalitarian on a social level, she knew, but on a sexual plane of being he wasn't capable of higher thought. She'd never met a man even remotely like him before, one that not only wanted to dominate her body, but was incapable of doing anything less. When Neil wanted to fuck he turned primal, animal, rational thought discarded. She loved it.

Valentina stood up, suddenly feeling a bit shy and nervous. She smiled inwardly at the incongruity, thinking to herself as she unzipped her jeans and stepped out of them that this man made her feel anything but jaded. Her shirt came off next, followed by her bra and thong panties. When she was finished undressing she reached towards him, her crimson-tipped nails honing in on his zipper.

He stilled her hand. Her golden brown head shot up, wondering at such an action.

"I'll take you when I'm ready," he said thickly, nudging her back towards the tent. "For now I want merely to look at you whilst you finish your work."

He wanted to enjoy being aroused, she thought, knowing he could fuck her when his urge became too great. She found her own body responding to his desires, her clit swelling as she went back down on all fours, face-first into the tent.

"Mmm very nice," he murmured. "Spread your legs a bit wider apart whilst you fix up the tent. All I want to see is ass, thighs, and bald cunt."

Valentina closed her eyes briefly at his words, intoxicating as they were. She imagined him staring at her swollen clit, at her puffed up labia, and felt liquid gather between her thighs as she did so. She knew his eyes were trained on her wet flesh, could almost feel them branding his name into her. She wanted him buried inside of her so badly that she ached for him, yet he didn't so much as touch her let alone mount her.

Five minutes later she announced to him that the tent was ready. "I'm done," she whispered, so aroused she could scarcely breathe let alone talk.

"Then come sit beside me on the blankets," he said hoarsely.

Valentina complied, her entire form emerging from the cover of the tent. She came down on her knees beside him, noticing at once that although he was still fully clothed, he had released his swollen erection from the confines of his jeans and was stroking it. It stood up as though carved of flesh-covered steel, so gloriously hard and stiff.

"May I suck on him?" she asked through passion-drunk eyes, meeting his gaze.

"In a minute," he murmured.

Neil reclined back on his elbows, his cock poking straight up. Craning his neck and upper torso, he leaned into Valentina and curled his tongue around one elongated nipple. She shuddered, pressing her breast closer to his face.

Drawing the nipple into his mouth, Neil sucked at it leisurely, pulling on it with his lips, rolling it around with his tongue, as he took her hand and guided it toward his scrotum, instructing her without words to massage him there.

He released the nipple on a groan, loving the feel of her silky hand gently toying with the tight balls inside of his sac. Falling onto his back, he placed his hands behind his neck to support the weight of his head, then watched her through glazed over eyes. "Suck on him, Tina," he murmured.

She obeyed, taking him hungrily into her mouth as though there was nothing else on the planet she wanted more. She paid special attention to the head of his cock, sucking vigorously at it, knowing that because he was like most European men and therefore uncircumcised he would be especially sensitive there.

"*Christ.*"

Neil gritted his teeth as his muscles instinctually clenched from the near-delirious pleasure. The sucking sounds her mouth made accompanied by the look of carnal enjoyment on her face made the hedonistic pleasure damn near painful.

Breathing heavily, he tried to forestall her erotic efforts with his hand so he could mount her body and empty himself inside of her, but when he attempted to do so her mouth merely latched onto him tighter and she began to suck on him faster and more briskly. Clearly, she meant for him to come in her mouth.

"Tina," he ground out, his muscles cording, his jugular vein bulging, "I'm coming, sweetheart."

That admission induced her sucking to become animalistic, moaning as her head bobbed up and down on his stiff erection. Long red nails wrapped around the base of his cock as full, swollen lips devoured the length of him, over and over, again and again.

"*Jesus.*"

Neil came on a groan, his eyes squinted shut, his teeth bared. He shouted out his satisfaction into the wilds of the Highlands, the echo reverberating throughout Cairn Gorm Mountain.

When Valentina had sucked him dry, depleted him of all that he had, her face bobbed up into his line of vision, looking utterly adorably and more than a little mischievous. She was pleased with herself he could tell, pleased that she'd driven him to such vocalized lengths.

Valentina grinned. "Wow, Neil. That shout could have put Tarzan to shame."

He half-laughed and half-groaned. "I'll work on perfecting my vine-swinging abilities a bit later."

She chuckled, coming down on the blanket to lie beside him. He gathered her close, kissing the top of her head. Wrapping her hand around his warm, flaccid penis, she sighed contentedly as her head came down on his chest. "I've never actually seen an uncircumcised cock before," she admitted with a smile in her voice.

"No?" He kissed the top of her head again. "American men are all circumcised?"

"For the most part, yeah." She grinned. "I've only read about men like you in books."

"In books, eh?" He considered that for a moment. "Is that also where you learned to suck an uncut man so well?" he asked, not meaning to be brisk but unable to waylay the possessiveness in his voice, "From a book?"

"Actually yes," she answered, unperturbed by his territorialism, reveling in it even.

Neil's heart began beating again. He released a breath as he kissed her forehead, pleased more than he cared to admit to by her answer. "Good."

They lay there in silence for a protracted moment, both of them simply enjoying holding each other after the intimacy they'd just shared. After a minute or two of this nonverbal bonding time it was Valentina who spoke first.

"You know," she said confessionally, for some reason or another wanting to share the most inane things with him, "I've been thinking for some time now that I'd like to try my hand at penning an historical novel."

One dark eyebrow shot up. He wondered why she'd been thinking of novels at a time like this. "I love the ones you write now. I'm certain you'll excel at whatever you try," he said truthfully.

Her head shot up. She searched his face. "You read my books?" she murmured.

He bent his neck a bit so he could kiss the tip of her nose. "Yes."

She smiled, strangely contented by his answer. None of her exes had ever taken the time to read her work, let alone enjoyed it. "The reason I brought the subject up to begin with is because I wanted you to know that when I write that historical I'm going to name the hero after you."

Neil's body stilled. He thought that the most wonderful compliment a woman had ever paid him. "I would be honored," he said, his brogue a murmur.

Valentina cleared her throat, realizing that the moment had grown too serious. She just wanted to enjoy Neil's company for the time being, not ponder all of these inexplicable feelings of affection she was developing towards him. "I wonder what I should name it," she said on a smile.

Neil sensed her shift in mood and let it go with good grace. He realized that now wasn't the time to push his own agenda onto her. And so, thinking on her statement a moment or two, he squeezed her gently and grinned. "How about, *You've Got Chain Mail*."

Valentina's light green eyes widened brilliantly right before she threw her head back and laughed. Neil smiled, secretly wondering if it was possible for a man to be any more content than he was at this very moment.

Chapter 6

The next two days were to be the happiest and most poignant hours of their lives. It was on top of this mountain, after all, where their affection for each other grew in unnatural leaps and bounds and both of them came to realize what it meant to truly care for and about another person.

Many, many years from now, when both of their heads were silvered and neither of them had a natural tooth left in their mouths, it would be back to the two days atop Cairn Gorm that their minds would forever wander, remembering the glory of having first discovered each other.

They wiled away those few precious hours on the mountain making love, taking long walks through the forest, eating meals over a campfire, and simply talking. Valentina's stories about what life was like growing up with two hippies for parents amused Neil to no end, while Neil's stories about his awkward childhood and adolescent years had the opposite effect on her and saddened Valentina for the pain life had unfairly dealt him. She never said as much to him, just held his hand and listened, sensing somehow that her silent affection and validation was all he needed or wanted.

But inevitably, just as all of life's magical moments do, their time on Cairn Gorm came to an end. Two days became one, one turned to none, and before they had quite realized the trip to Paradise was over, they were side by side in Neil's Lexus headed back to Edinburgh...and to reality.

Neil couldn't quite squelch the brewing restlessness that stemmed from not knowing what would happen between the two of them when they returned to civilization. He wondered what she'd think of his sensible, ordinary life, and of the pretentious, stuffy professorial acquaintances he was forever forced to endure at one university function or another.

Little did he know, Valentina was staring out the passenger side window worrying her lip as she fretted over the same thing, though with a different twist. She was wondering whether or not Neil had room in his life for a feisty, passionate artist type when his own life was already so well structured and so visibly lacking in the very characteristics that comprised her personality.

Perhaps that had been on purpose, she thought somewhat sadly. Perhaps he had looked at his time with her as a rendezvous and no more. Perhaps when they reached Edinburgh he wouldn't want anything more to do with her.

Half an hour later, the Lexus cruised down Princes Street and came to a halt in front of The Balmoral. Neil's eyes flicked over the hotel where Valentina was staying before flicking back to her. "Well," he said, trying his best to tamper the sound of disappointment he was certain was laced in his voice, "we're here."

Valentina smiled over to him as she opened the passenger side door. "Thanks for the ride." She grinned. "Thanks for everything. I had a terrific time."

"So did I." Neil's gaze fell to her lap, his dark eyes taking one last appreciative sweep over her fertile form. He took a deep breath and expelled it on a resolved sigh. A woman like her, so vital and full of life, would never be happy with a man like him, a man who for all intent and purposes was her antithesis.

She might enjoy him for another day or two, perhaps even for the whole of her stay in Scotland, but inevitably she would leave him and he wasn't altogether certain he'd be able to deal with it. He was going to have a difficult enough of a time returning to his mundane existence as it was.

"Thank you for a memorable weekend, Tina." He cleared his throat. "I shall always look back upon it fondly."

Valentina's light green eyes clashed with his. He thought for a stunned moment that she looked a bit sad, but then a moment later a beautiful smile was fixed on her face and he decided he'd been imagining things.

"So will I," she said softly.

Unable to resist, Neil reached across the space that separated them and kissed her gently on the lips. She kissed him back, sweeping her tongue inside of his mouth, brushing it against his own. And then, almost as if by magic, she had retreated from the Lexus and was gone.

Neil watched Valentina walk into the hotel, feeling more lonely and miserable than he'd ever felt before. He sighed. He couldn't shake the feeling that he'd just lost the best thing that had ever happened to him.

Chapter 7

"You look as though somebody just killed your best friend."

Neil's head shot up at the sound of his friend and colleague's voice. Seated behind his desk inside of his office at university, he waved a hand at the empty seat across from him, indicating he could sit there. "Good morning, John. I haven't seen you since you left on holiday to Rome. How was the trip?"

"Brilliant." John Hastings, outfitted in the same sensible lecturer's attire of tweed trousers, formal shirt, and suit jacket that Neil was wearing, nodded toward his friend as he shrugged his trousers up at the knee and took a seat. "I'm teaching a class on Roman law this term so the trip will come in handy. I spent a few days touring the legal libraries there, seeing the antiquities firsthand. It was excellent."

Neil thought it sounded vastly boring in comparison to the three days in Eden he'd spent, but declined to say as much. No use in detracting from John's fine mood just because his own had been in the sewers for the past three Valentina-less days. "I'm glad you had a terrific time then."

"As am I." John studied his face for a moment or two before saying anything else. He threw a hand toward him as he nestled further into the seat. "Okay. What gives?"

Surprised, Neil glanced up. It occurred to him that he probably appeared to be somewhat distracted. Not that he wasn't. "What do you mean?"

John sighed. "Come on, man. I've known you since we went to university together. What's going on? Why do you look so damn depressed?"

"I look depressed?" he asked, hoping he seemed surprised.

In reaction, John merely sighed again.

"All right, all right," Neil said, doing a little sighing of his own. He pushed the gold-wire spectacles up the bridge of his nose and regarded his oldest friend. He shook his head, trying to downplay the situation a bit. "It's a woman."

"A woman?" John studied his features curiously. "Margaret hardly seems the sort to bring a man low. No offense to the mouse, but I—"

"I'm not speaking of Margaret. She dumped me a week ago as a matter of fact."

John's eyebrows shot up. He leaned in closer to Neil's desk and grinned. "The mouse worked up the nerve to dump you, eh? Do tell. And whilst you're at it make certain you tell me of this other woman." His grin was infectious. "I want details."

Neil shook his head at his friend's odd humor, but gave him the details he sought. He told him about meeting Valentina in Jenners department store, about Margaret calling an end to their relationship that very afternoon, and about having worked up the nerve to follow Valentina Jason-Elliot up to Strathy Point.

Twenty minutes later, the story having been brought to a conclusion in front of the Balmoral, John steepled his fingertips together and regarded him. "I'm amazed," he confessed.

Neil snorted his agreement. "As am I." He sighed. "I can't believe that I had the nerve to follow her in the first place, let alone—"

"That's not what amazes me." John grinned. "Though it does set one back a bit."

Neil looked at him quizzically. "Then what precisely is it that you find so amazing?"

The expression on his colleague's face indicated that he should already have known the answer. "That you let her walk out of your life so easily, of course. You didn't even attempt to see if things could have gone further."

"For what reason, John?" He chuckled self-depreciatingly. "I'm hardly a man that leads an exciting lifestyle. Can you imagine someone like Valentina Jason-Elliot, given all I've told you about her and her lifestyle, being happy in the long run with a lecturer of mathematics?"

"And why the bloody hell not," John answered incredulously. "Not a damn thing wrong with that."

"It is boring," Neil said distinctly, over-enunciating each word. "I am boring." He waved a hand dismissively. "Let us discuss this no more. I'm trying to simply push the weekend's events from my mind and continue on as before."

John sighed, shaking his head slightly. "If that's truly your wish…" His voice had been inflected as he'd spoke, indicating he didn't really believe Neil wanted it that way.

"Of course I don't wish for it," he bit out, "but neither am I prone to indulging in an overactive fantasy life."

"It sounds to me like you're scared."

"I resent that! I am not scared!"

"No?" John's brow drew together disbelievingly. "Then pick up the phone and give her a call."

Neil didn't know what to say to that. He glanced toward his desktop and began absently toying with two paperclips laying atop it. "I'm certain she's busy," he mumbled.

"Uh-huh."

His nostrils flared. "I am not scared," Neil gritted out. "I am merely...realistic."

"Uh-huh."

"Oh bloody hell but I wish you'd quit saying that!"

John scooted closer to the desk. "You know what I think?"

"No. But I'm certain I'm about to be made privy."

"Don't be so sarcastic, Dr. Macalister." John inclined his head succinctly. "I think that woman seems larger than life to you, and you're letting the fear that she couldn't possibly entertain the notion of falling for an ordinary lecturer of mathematics rot your brain. What you're forgetting, however, is that she's just a person like anybody else."

Neil rolled his eyes. "Thank you for that riveting commentary on my sordid mental state. I shall cherish it always."

John sighed, standing up. "Hey, I tried."

Neil watched him walk away, feeling decidedly wretched. It hadn't been necessary to snap at his oldest friend simply because they weren't on agreement in the matter of one Valentina Jason-Elliot. "John?"

"Yes?" He turned around and regarded him.

"Thank you." He smiled. "I shall think on your words."

"You're welcome." John grinned as he opened the office door. "Let's just hope you take my advice and give her a call."

* * * * *

Later that evening inside of his flat, Neil broodingly stared at the phone, sensing it was his fate to pick up the damn thing, yet also sensing he'd hate the outcome of having done so. "Shite," he muttered as he reached for the receiver and pounded out the number to the Balmoral on the keypad.

He was an idiot, he decided. A damned, fool idiot.

"Balmoral. How may I direct your call?"

He cleared his throat, already feeling nervous even though he was currently only speaking to one of the hotel's staff. "Valentina Jason-Elliot's room, please."

"I'm sorry but that's a blocked line. I can only put the call through if your name is on her list of approved callers. What's your name, sir?"

Neil sighed, his heart plummeting. "Neil Macalister, but I'm certain I'm not—"

"I see your name, Dr. Macalister. One moment and I'll put the call through."

Neil was too stunned to react. He wasn't given any time to adjust to that potentially telling piece of information either, for a moment later a certain Georgia peach was drawling over the connection, her smoky voice giving him an instant erection. "Hello?"

Neil opened his mouth to speak, but nothing came out.

"Hello?" she asked again.

Neil's mind flew in a thousand different directions as he tried to come up with a plausible excuse for having called, and hopefully one that didn't sound overly pathetic. He cleared his throat. "Tina? This is Neil."

"Hi, Neil!"

Was that excitement he heard in her voice? He restlessly shifted in the chair, his erection broaching painful. "Something occurred to me after I dropped you off at the hotel a few days ago and I was hoping we could discuss it."

"Oh? And what was that?"

Yes—what *was* that? he asked himself grimly. He'd never been very good at winging it, so to speak, but at the moment he supposed he was performing even less stellar than usual. "We uh…we…"

"Yes?"

"We didn't use any manner of protection." Hey, come to think of it they really hadn't. He warmed to his topic, deciding it was the perfect, plausible excuse to call. He cleared his throat. "I wanted to assure you that I am in sound health with no manner of disease at all."

Valentina gasped. "My God, I can't believe it slipped my mind! I've never behaved so recklessly in my entire life," she said as if she couldn't quite believe it. "Thank you for calling to let me know. I'm sure that eventually I would have realized it too and worried. Oh and by the way, it's the same with me. I have a clean bill of health."

Well, Neil thought gloomily, there was the end of that conversation. "I never doubted it."

"I guess I should also have mentioned that I'm on the pill, so there's no worry that I'll become pregnant either."

Neil wished that news cheered him up, but he found that it only served to make him feel that much worse. "Excellent." He sighed, unable to think of a damned thing else to say. He decided that if he could work up the nerve to call her again he'd come prepared with crib notes the next time. "Well," he said, "I suppose I should go, then."

She hesitated for a moment. "Thank you for calling."

"Certainly." He fidgeted with the phone cord. "Goodbye then."

"Goodbye."

Neil hung up the phone, feeling a curious mix of excitement and depression. Excitement because he'd spoken with her again, depression because he now knew with all certainty that she wouldn't be pounding on his door any time soon, pregnant and demanding he do the honorable thing by marrying her.

He frowned. Goddamned, bloody, fucking birth control pills.

Chapter 8

Valentina sat inside the Ballast tent that had been erected within the boundaries of the Edinburgh Festival with the other Ballast authors, signing autographs and doing her best to sell copies of *The Scream* before her next release hit stands at month's end. Her head shot up when her peripheral vision snagged a pair of camel tweed trousers, but was disappointed when she found them attached to a blond-haired man instead of one certain dark-haired man she couldn't seem to let go of. The stranger was handsome, but he wasn't Neil.

It had been four days since he'd called, a week since she'd last seen him. Unfortunately, time wasn't helping to ease her sense of loss at all.

"I was hoping I might get an autograph." The blond man smiled down to her. "I've already got this book, but what the hell, another copy won't put me in the poorhouse."

Valentina grinned. "Glad to hear it. Who do I make it out to?"

"John Hastings." He smiled, watching her eyes for a reaction. "I'm a friend and colleague of Neil Macalister's."

He wasn't disappointed. Her light green eyes widened fractionally, tellingly he thought, before she returned her gaze to the book.

"And how is he doing?" she asked a tad too nonchalantly as she scribbled onto the book.

"Like shite," he said bluntly. Valentina's head popped up and John grinned at her. "So if there's even a miniscule chance that you're feeling the same, perhaps you should give him a call."

She searched his eyes. "Did Neil send you here today?"

"No."

Her heart fell with John's admission.

"Truth be told I live just around the corner and decided to come out for a wee stroll. When I saw the Ballast tent I figured I'd pop in and say hello."

She sighed, handing him the autographed book. "What makes you think Neil wants me to call him?"

"As I said, he feels like shite. Has ever since the day your little—" he cleared his throat, "—rendezvous came to an end."

"Really?" she asked quietly.

John chuckled. "Yeah, really." He looked at his watch then glanced back to her. "If you can take a few minutes break, I'd be happy to buy you a drink and tell you all about it."

Valentina grinned. She nodded, then slowly rose to her feet. "You've got it."

* * * * *

"I'm stunned." Absently swirling her White Russian around in the glass, Valentina met John's gaze. "I've been walking around depressed for an entire week thinking he didn't want heads or tails to do with me. And now you show up and tell me it's because he thinks he's boring?" She shook her head, mystified. "If there is one thing Neil is definitely not it's boring. Where did he get an idea like that?"

John chuckled as he set his glass of wine down on the pub's tabletop. "Men are notoriously odd creatures. We can't seem to help it."

She grinned at that, feeling more lighthearted than she had in days. "I owe you big time. If it wasn't for you I never would have known any of this. Neil didn't seem at all inclined toward wanting to see me again which is why I didn't push the issue."

"And now?"

Her smile was slow and full of mischief. "And now I'm going to prove to Dr. Macalister that he's anything but dull and sensible."

John raised his glass of wine in salute. He grinned. "I'm afraid when all is said and done I'm going to have to press Neil for the sinful details."

She toasted him with the White Russian. "They should be good ones. I have a flair for the dramatic. Can't seem to help it." She chuckled. "It runs in the family."

Chapter 9

Neil pushed his gold-wire spectacles up the bridge of his nose as he took to the lecture hall. His eyes swept dispassionately over the bevy of students, noting at once that he had a full house of thirty of more. He opened his briefcase as he arrived at the podium and retrieved the class roster from it. "James O'Donnell."

"Present."

"Marion McKenna."

"Present."

And on he went for another thirty or so names until he reached the end of the list. "Have I missed anyone?" he asked as he pushed his spectacles up the bridge of his nose again.

A hand went up in his peripheral vision. "Mine."

"And your name?" he asked as he glanced up. "What is your—"

Neil's breath caught in the back of his throat when he realized just who the mystery student was. She wasn't behaving as though anything out of the ordinary was happening. Hell, she wasn't acting as though she even recognized him.

Valentina was dressed in a wantonly tight shirt that showcased her impressive bosom and the outline of her nipples, as well as a tight little skirt that came up to the tops of her thighs. The completely white ensemble was finished off with a pair of high-heeled shoes, shoes that would put her close to his six-foot frame in height while standing. "What is your name?" he asked as calmly as possible.

"Valentina Jason-Elliot."

"Fine." Why was she here? he asked himself. What was she doing? He pretended to record her name, his heart beating quite dramatically in his chest. "I've added you to the roster."

It took supreme effort, but somehow or another Neil managed to commence his lecture. Turning to the blackboard, he began scribbling out names and dates, giving the students a brief history of mathematics. Well, he thought grimly as he continued to scribble, if she hadn't thought him a complete and utter bore before this moment, she no doubt would after hearing him pontificate on the usefulness of calculus to the sciences.

"And so," he droned on as he returned to the podium and continued his lecture, "the way for differential and inferential calculus was paved by Sir Isaac Newton…" His lips kept working, spewing out dates and facts, but his mind was in turmoil and because of that fact his gaze flicked toward the one causing it.

Neil watched in fascination and shock—unable to do anything to stop her, unable to call attention away from himself—as Valentina slowly parted her thighs, revealing the fact that she was wearing no panties. Wet, bald flesh glistened from the first row of desks and he had to look away to keep from making a fool of himself. His penis was so stiff he feared it might explode.

He continued his lecture, not moving away from the podium this time for fear a student might see his stiff erection. "Following Sir Isaac Newton's thesis…" He deserved a medal for his fortitude, for being able to resist looking at her, he thought to himself.

But, of course, Neil could only take the suspense so long. He had to know what she was up to, had to see for himself what she was now doing. Against his will, his eyes strayed once more to Valentina's desk, widening upon their discovery.

She was playing with herself. Right there at the desk. Right across from him as he lectured. It occurred to him that she had planned her seating well, off to the right as she was, for she was able to reach down and masturbate her glorious cunt without making any but him the wiser.

Blood-red fingernails slithered around her labial folds, opening them wide for his inspection. She drew her swollen clit between her index and middle fingers, poking it out for him to see, as she began to work it around in a circular motion. Her light green eyes were glazed over as she looked up at him, boldly meeting his gaze as she sat there in the lecture hall and masturbated.

And somehow he continued to talk, somehow he continued to draw the attention of the class toward himself and keep it there, somehow he managed to keep glancing away from that scrumptiously wet cunt long enough to keep suspicion at bay. "…which resulted in the implementation of the calculus we use today…"

He didn't know how he kept a poker face, didn't know how he managed to refrain from breaking out into a sweat, for all it took was one glimpse of her pussy and he had reverted right back into the primal mode he'd spent that entire wondrous weekend in. "If you would turn now to page…"

Somehow or another he got through the lecture, managed to act as though nothing was amiss for another twenty minutes, even as Valentina played with her flesh the entire time. She never once stopped, he noted, not until he called an end to the class and told them he'd see them on Wednesday.

"Ms. Jason-Elliot," he announced, amazed he sounded so calm. "I would like you to stay after class so we can discuss your schedule this term."

"Of course," she answered, sounding for all the world as though there was nothing out of the ordinary going on.

By the time the last student had filed out of the lecture hall and he'd shut and locked the door behind them, Neil had withstood as much torture as he could take. He prowled toward the desk Valentina had occupied without saying a word, absently noting that she was now standing next to it rather than sitting.

Unzipping his trousers, he released his stiff erection in one motion and raised her short skirt up to her hips in the next. His eyes flicked broodingly over her clean-shaven pussy as his hands lifted her tight little top up over her breasts, freeing them for his palms. She gasped as he cupped them, her eyes narrowing in desire as his thumbs brushed over the nipples.

"Turn around," he said softly but forcibly.

He released her breasts as she obeyed him, allowing her to turn around in a half-circle and spread her legs apart so he could rut in her from behind. She bent over the desk as far as she could, closing her eyes in anticipation as she raised her buttocks into the air.

Valentina gasped as his long, thick cock surged into her wet flesh from behind. "*Neil.*" She moaned as he took her, groaning when he cupped her breasts from behind and played with her nipples while he fucked her.

Neil gritted his teeth as he rode her body, pumping in and out of her tight hole in long, agonizing strokes. His fingers tugged at and tweaked her nipples as he slammed into her, again and again, wringing her body of orgasm after orgasm.

"*Oh God.*"

"Does my cock feel good?" he murmured into her ear, his balls slapping against her as he pounded into her hard. "Does it?" he ground out, his jaw clenched.

"*Yes.*"

Neil tugged at her nipples again, pulling them in the way she liked as a reward for her answer. She moaned, causing him to rut deeper and faster.

"Has my pussy been bad this week?" he asked almost casually as he surged into her again and again. "Has it fucked anyone else?"

"*No.*" She met his thrusts, gluttonously loving every moment of it.

He rotated his hips and slammed home hard, his fingers still pulling and tweaking her elongated nipples. "I'll give you more cock then," he growled, "since you've been a good girl whilst away from me."

He lived up to his word, driving his stiff shaft into her over and over, again and again, making her come more times and more violently than she'd previously thought possible.

Valentina closed her eyes and smiled, wanting him to go on fucking her forever, wanting him to slam into her for hour after hour, but sensed that his orgasm was drawing near. She met his thrusts greedily, slapping her buttocks back at him, moaning as he wrung her pussy into sopping wet flesh.

"*Tina.*"

And then he was coming, groaning as he surged into her for a final time. He released her breasts, grabbing at her hips and digging into them with his fingers, as he spurted his orgasm deep inside of her body.

Neil could scarcely breathe let alone move, so he kept her there for a protracted moment, pinned to the desk and joined to him at the flesh while he regained his senses.

When he let her up a moment later, she whirled around and regarded him, a smile tugging at her lips. She looked adorably wanton, he thought, her wide luminous eyes an innocent contrast against the top that had been shoved up over her breasts and the skirt that rode around her hips.

"The spectacles are an arousing touch, Neil, but I think next time you should remove them." She made to break away from him. "No sense in getting them broken."

Next time? he thought hopefully.

She pulled her tight white top down to conceal her breasts, then did the same with the skirt, hiding her bald cunt from his view. "You have another lecture in an hour, don't you? At least that's what John said. You better prepare for it."

Neil shook his head to clear it. He was having a hard time getting back into lecture mode when the woman of his dreams had just sauntered into his hall, seduced him and fucked him mindless. "Y-Yes," he stammered out, reigning in his thoughts. "Yes, of course."

She smiled, slinging her purse over her shoulder as she strolled towards the door. "See you later then."

"Later?" He cleared his throat as he put his sated penis back into his trousers and zipped up. "When later?"

Valentina's hand stilled on the doorknob. She regarded him from over her shoulder as she made to open it. "Soon."

He nodded.

"Oh and Neil," she said as she opened the door, stopping when it was half ajar. "One more thing."

He searched her eyes. "Yes?"

"You are anything but boring." She smiled slowly. "But if you call what we just did dull then feel free to bore me to tears any time."

Neil watched her leave, realizing that somehow or another John had found her and spoken with her. There was no other explanation.

A grin tugging at the corners of his lips, he removed the gold-wire spectacles from his face and tossed them into the trashcan as he strode from the lecture hall.

Chapter 10

"Bloody hell." Neil muttered under his breath as he fished his spectacles out of the trash bin. He supposed he should have waited to complete the symbolic gesture of casting off the old and starting anew until after he was done lecturing for the day.

He'd realized almost from the onset of his last class that he wasn't able to make out his own chicken scratches without visual aid. He had a final class left today and the contact lenses he'd worn to the Highlands were back at his flat.

Neil retrieved the spectacles, thankfully noting that no trash of any sort had been thrown on top of them. Hopelessly fastidious, nevertheless, he couldn't stop himself from taking them to the gentlemen's washroom and giving them a thorough cleansing.

As he stood in front of the sink and dried the lenses, he glanced up at himself in the mirror. Pushing the gold-wire spectacles up the bridge of his nose, he noticed for the first time that they no longer looked right on him.

He had changed. She had changed him. Nothing was the same anymore and it never would be again.

He smiled to himself, realizing that he didn't mind that fact. Then he frowned, wondering what precisely that meant and whether or not Valentina Jason-Elliot intended to be a permanent part of this new life.

* * * * *

Seated at a table inside of her hotel room, Valentina sipped thoughtfully from a glass of Merlot as she considered her next move. When she had first decided to go to the university this morning, a tiny tremor of doubt had assailed her before she'd seen the seduction through. If John had been wrong in his assumptions, after all, she would have felt like a fool.

But no. John had been right. Neil still wanted her. She was sure of that now. The problem as she saw it was getting a certain stubborn lecturer of mathematics to realize that they were made for each other.

She didn't want doubts between them, didn't want him constantly wondering if the bond they'd formed in the Highlands had been a fluke. She wanted him, all of him, and she wanted him to long for her so badly that he'd overcome all reservations to the contrary and seek her out.

So she'd decided to seduce him...and to keep seducing him until he couldn't stand the thought of a day going by without seeing her. She'd know the mission was accomplished when he could no longer wait for her to come to him and he hied off to find her instead.

With most men such a gesture would have been meaningless, but with Neil she realized it was just the opposite. When he came to her, when he could no longer bear the separation, that was when she'd know he was hers — hook, line, and sinker.

Valentina raised the glass of wine to her lips and sipped slowly. She was going to seduce him again. It was just a question of when and how.

Chapter 11

Two evenings later, formally dressed in a tuxedo jacket and kilt, Neil made small talk with the mathematics colleague seated to his right inside the University of Edinburgh's banquet hall. He couldn't wait for the boring meal to come to an end, wanting as he was to go back to his flat and sort out his tumultuous thoughts in privacy.

He had thought Valentina would want nothing to do with him after their return from Cairn Gorm, but he had been wrong once. She had come to him and seduced him in his own lecture hall. But then she had disappeared and he hadn't heard from her since. He wasn't certain what to make of that.

After that morning two days ago when he had taken her over the desk, Neil had driven by her hotel room that night and contemplated going in. But he hadn't. In the end, indecisive as to what he should do, he had merely sat in the car, broodingly staring out of the Lexus window, his emotions all over the place.

He was changing, life was changing. He felt like a prisoner trying to decide whether or not to attempt a jailbreak.

"Ah, there you are. And I see you saved me a seat."

Neil sighed a breath of relief, grateful that John Hastings had at last shown up. His arrival gave Neil the perfect excuse to quit chatting it up with the boring professor seated to the right of him. "Hello, John. It's good of you to have finally made it," he said pointedly.

"It's not like any of us has a choice," John said under his breath as he took the seat to Neil's left. He plastered on a smile as he inclined his head toward the wife of a tenured professor. "Duty calls."

"Mmm yes." Neil grinned, meeting his friend's gaze. "Nothing quite like a university function to slow down an already dull day I always say."

"It's about to get duller." John sighed. "Professor Hamilton is approaching the podium."

"Oh joy," Neil said dryly. "I hope he tells us the story of how he made Queen Elizabeth's acquaintance whilst in London. We've only heard it...what? Eighteen or nineteen times."

John chuckled softly, then winced as Professor Hamilton began to speak. "Looks like twenty."

Left with no choice, both men turned their attention toward the podium and listened as Hamilton droned on. Neil found his mind wandering, a natural reaction to sheer and utter boredom he supposed.

As his thoughts scattered, he found them solidifying around the enigma of one particular woman. He couldn't help but to consider what Valentina was currently doing. And just as importantly, whom she was doing it with.

Neil became so lost in his thoughts that it took his brain a suspended moment to register the fact that something out of the ordinary was happening, something he hadn't been expecting at all. And that the something was occurring right at his table...

Or, more to the point, right *under* his table.

Neil held himself steady, beads of perspiration breaking out on his brow, as a very warm and wanton mouth wrapped itself around his cock and took him all the way in. He knew that mouth well for it had sucked him off many times before, sinfully delicious in its skill. He could be blindfolded with a thousand different women taking turns giving him pleasure and he'd still be able to pick out a blowjob from Valentina without any difficulty at all.

As inconspicuously as possible, Neil glanced down toward his lap, brushed aside the tablecloth a tad, and saw a long pink tongue dart out from between a pair of crimson-stained lips to lick around his sensitive head. He turned poker-hard in an instant.

Setting the tablecloth back in place, Neil took a deep breath as his gaze flicked around the room and he considered how in the hell he would possibly survive this banquet. He could feel the cum building up in his balls, knew he was going to shoot a huge load. He could even feel his breathing growing labored, his heart rate over the top, though he did the best job he could to steady it.

Neil's eyes briefly closed as Valentina began deep-throating him. His nostrils flared. He could feel her lips around the base of his cock, feel them stroking upwards in a smooth slide, feel them stopping at the head and sucking briskly at it. He felt his toes curl and his muscles clench as he did the best job he could do to keep from groaning aloud.

From the right, Professor Atchinson mumbled something or another to Neil under his breath. All he could do was smile and nod back before turning away from him to face the podium once more in an effort to somewhat shield his facial expressions.

He swiped the sweat from his brow as Valentina's hands began to massage the muscles in his thighs. He took a deep breath as she paused to nibble at his head, then resumed her sucking.

She turned animalistic then, sucking on his cock in a fast up and down motion. Voracious. Greedy. Wanting his cum, wanting him to burst in her mouth right there under the table.

Her sucking became faster, faster, and faster still. Neil closed his eyes and breathed deeply, praying for once that

Hamilton would keep on talking so that all eyes would remain trained on him up at the podium.

The sucking intensified around the head of his cock, all of Valentina's considerable skill focused on that one highly sensitive area of his manhood. Fingers joined in to massage his balls and Neil knew that he was inevitably close to coming.

He could imagine what she looked like, could see her golden brown head bobbing up and down on his shaft in his mind's eye. He knew the look of carnal rapture that would be intrinsic to her facial features, knew what those puffy red lips would look like as they feasted on him. It was all he could take.

Hamilton's speech came to a finale and applause broke out just in time to muffle the small groan Neil wasn't able to suppress. He spurted into her awaiting mouth once, twice, three times, a seemingly endless eruption of sperm, as his muscles tightly clenched and his jaw went rigid.

"Thank God that's over," John muttered from beside him. "That was a bloody boring speech."

Neil took a deep breath to steady himself. He had come so hard he felt ready to black out. And now she was sucking at the tiny hole on his cock, her lips and tongue greedily cleaning him dry. He gritted his teeth. "Boring—right."

Chapter 12

Neil awoke the next morning with a rigid hard-on. Stumbling out of bed naked, he wished a certain woman was lying next to him so she could take care of matters for him. But she wasn't. Just as she had the morning she'd seduced him in the lecture hall, so too had she disappeared after sucking him half to death at last evening's banquet.

She hadn't stopped at one blowjob. She had gone on to give him another. It still amazed him that at almost forty he could get so hard so quickly and produce such vast quantities of cum for this one incredibly arousing woman.

Prowling into the bathroom, Neil flipped on the shower and stepped under it, quickly washing his body and shampooing his hair. He had some work to take care of in the office today, though lord knew it was going to be difficult at best and impossible at worst to keep his brain tuned to mathematics.

Turning off the water, he toweled himself dry, careful not to hurt himself in the process. His erection was quite large and painfully swollen. Slinging the towel over his shoulder, Neil padded back into the bedroom, his thoughts in chaos.

He wanted to go to her, wanted to find her. He needed her.

It was more than just sex that he desired from Valentina, more than mounting her body and riding her flesh into oblivion. He wanted all of her...heart, soul, as well as body. He wanted what they'd shared on Cairn Gorm and he wanted it to last forever.

But would he make her happy in the long run? he asked himself for the umpteenth time. Could a twenty-nine-year-old passionate woman possibly remain happy living out her life with a reserved lecturer of mathematics ten years her senior?

These thoughts continued to plague him as he left the flat and made his way to university. There were so many questions, so many damned doubts, but he also knew totally and completely that there was only one answer.

He had to have her, regardless to anything else. He had to find a way to keep her at his side.

Neil withdrew his office key from his trousers' pocket, preparing to unlock the door. The door swung open at his touch, however, so he stepped inside, deciding he must have forgotten to lock up before he'd retired home last night. The sight that greeted him made him stop in his tracks.

"Hi."

The erection Neil had sustained all morning grew that much more pronounced as his eyes feasted on the reclining form of a very naked Valentina Jason-Elliot. She was lying on the small sofa in his office, the one opposite his desk, her legs spread wide, her bald cunt glistening.

Her breasts were thrust upward in invitation, the nipples already stabbing up from their puffy pink bases. She was simply lying there, wearing nothing but a mischievous smile, her legs splayed submissively wide for his thrusts.

"Hi." Neil's eyes burned possessively into hers as he closed the door behind him and began unbuttoning his shirt.

"I was going to wait until tonight," she admitted, her light green eyes hooded in desire, "but I found that I couldn't." She watched in anticipation as his muscled body emerged from the clothes.

"I'm glad you didn't," he murmured, "because I need to fuck you right now."

And then she was reaching out for him, pulling him down on top of her as he settled himself between her thighs and surged into her in a single, powerful thrust. He could offer her no foreplay, no words of affection, for his mind had long since gone primal and his body had taken over in its need to mate with hers.

Valentina gasped as he entered her, clutching the back of his shoulders as her legs wrapped around his waist. Her head fell back on a moan as he slammed into her hard, bringing her to the brink of orgasm.

She could hear her flesh slurping up his cock, could hear him groaning as he pounded away into oblivion, mindless of everything save the body he was claiming. His hands found her breasts, cupping them and forcing them up and close together so he could suck on her nipples while he fucked her.

"*Neil.*"

Valentina climaxed, her back arching and her nipples poking up into his warm mouth, stiffer than before. He groaned, sucking the peaks more vigorously, surging into her sticky flesh in fast, deep strokes. Her legs continued to cling to his waist, affording him a deep penetration that aroused them both to a fevered pitch.

His mouth firmly latched onto a jutting nipple, he moaned against her breast as he came. His entire body convulsing, Neil violently erupted into her, spurting his hot cum deep inside of her womb.

He could feel her hands roaming over his back, massaging his buttocks as his breathing steadied and his eyelids grew heavy. He didn't let go of the nipple, wouldn't let go of the nipple. His head fell onto her breast, still drawing from it.

Chapter 13

"Oh Cynthia, please tell me you're joking."

"'Fraid not." Her sigh could be heard clearly across the telephone connection. "That worthless bastard left my ass."

Valentina chewed on her bottom lip as she clutched the phone firmly in her palm. "Oh sweetheart, I'm so sorry. I never realized the two of you were having problems. You and Osmond seemed as though you were meant for each other."

"Looks can apparently be deceiving. As we speak, my husband is moving in with the cover model from his latest novel."

"Oh dear." Valentina closed her eyes briefly, feeling Cynthia's pain as if it were her own. The two of them had been the closest of friends ever since they'd met at a dinner party hosted by Ballast Books. Both women wrote for the publishing company, though in different departments.

"What am I going to do, girl?" Cynthia sighed. "To be honest, I haven't been in love with Os for years, but he's still my husband. I'm so depressed I can barely see straight."

Valentina pondered that for a moment. "Well," she said, clearing her throat, "why don't you come over to Scotland and stay with me for the next week?" She smiled, thinking it a truly wonderful idea. "Not only would I love tooling around with you, but if you hadn't been so worried about what that jerk would think of you vacationing in Europe in the first place then you'd be here anyway. As a matter of fact, you're *supposed* to be over here with the rest of the Ballast authors."

"That's true," Cynthia agreed, sounding as though she was warming to the idea.

"You could stay right here with me. Ballast set me up in a nice room."

"Forget it." Cynthia chuckled, her first sign of good humor since she'd called Valentina's room a little over twenty minutes ago. "No offense, Tina, but the last thing I'm in the mood to do is listen to you be all lovey-dovey with that guy you met."

Valentina frowned. "Have you ever known me to be the lovey-dovey type?" She refused to think about the mushy feelings she harbored for Neil. "Besides, he's never even been up to my hotel room."

"Uh-huh. So you haven't slept with Dr. Stud then?"

"I didn't say that," she mumbled.

Cynthia threw her head back and laughed. "Never mind, girl. Now I really don't want to know."

Valentina chuckled, shaking her head slightly. "Just say you'll come. Bring Erica if you want. Just please say it's okay for me to call the front desk and reserve you a room?" she asked hopefully.

Cynthia was quiet for so long that Valentina was certain she was going to say no. But then, miraculously, she did an about-face and changed her mind. "I can't bring my daughter because school will be starting soon, but I'm sure my mother will keep her for me. It is a working vacation after all."

"Then..."

"Yes." Cynthia chuckled, feeling more wicked and brazen than she had in ages. "Go ahead and reserve that room. For one week."

Valentina grinned, unable to believe she'd managed to convince her. "Excellent. I'll call downstairs right now. Book that flight as soon as we hang up!"

"I will, honey. Thanks for everything." Her voice took on a tremulous note, letting Valentina know she was getting excited about the idea. "If there's a seat on tonight's flight I'll be there tomorrow morning."

"I can't wait."

"Me neither! See you then."

As Valentina hung up the phone, it occurred to her that a week wasn't a very long time, not very long at all. And yet that's all the time she had left with Neil. One more week and she'd be headed back for Atlanta. The thought was depressing in the extreme.

For the past seven days, ever since the evening of Neil's formal university reception, she had been seducing him in new ways almost every day. She'd made herself available to him in his office, sneaked into his flat and made love to him there, she'd even lured him to Sterling Castle and rode him into ecstasy on the palace grounds.

And yet, after all of her effort, Neil still hadn't sought her out.

Valentina stood up with a sigh and strolled over to gaze down upon her view of Edinburgh from the window. Crossing her arms over her breasts, she wondered if all of her planning and plotting had been in vain. Perhaps Neil was content to have an affair with her while she was here, but maybe he truly didn't want to continue things beyond her remaining scheduled week.

He knew she was planning to leave, knew that her tickets back to Atlanta were a week from today. He hadn't said anything to try and thwart those plans. Nothing at all.

Valentina slumped down in the nearest chair and took a deep breath. She had the same nervous feeling in her belly that she'd had while waiting on Ballast to get back to her concerning whether or not they planned to buy her first manuscript. Only this time, she conceded, the stakes were a hell of a lot higher.

* * * * *

The next evening Neil sat in his Lexus, broodingly staring up at the Balmoral. This was the second day straight that Valentina had not come to him. All last night and today he'd been walking on eggshells, wondering what new erotic situation she had devised for him to partake of. He'd waited at his flat tonight for her until after ten o'clock in the evening and then, unable to bear it any longer, had gotten in his car and drove over to her hotel.

So now here he sat, wondering whether or not he should go upstairs, wondering whether or not she would be pleased by such a move on his part or wishing he'd leave her the hell alone. Perhaps she hadn't shown up for a rendezvous these past two days because she'd decided she wanted nothing further to do with him. She was scheduled to leave in a week. Perhaps she wanted a clean break.

And perhaps he wouldn't let her get away so easily.

Neil's fingers gripped the steering wheel so harshly that his knuckles turned white. He was tired of playing Mr. Nice Guy, sick to death of letting life happen to him instead of taking what he wanted from it, consequences be damned. He had been raised to be a considerate gentleman, for all the nothingness that had brought to him. Well, no more.

He wanted Valentina, needed her even. Nothing was the same anymore. Hell, he didn't even dress as he used to. Gone were the gold spectacles, gone was the sensible lecturer's attire outside of university, gone was everything he had ever called normal.

Glancing down at the snug-fitting black jeans and polo shirt he wore, Neil arrived at an irrevocable conclusion. If Valentina hadn't figured out by now that she would never be going back to Atlanta then she was about to figure it out tonight.

Wrenching open the car door, he smoothly alighted from it, his steps determined. Making his way into the Balmoral he bypassed the lobby entirely and headed straight for her suite upstairs.

When he got out of the elevator on the fifth floor, he perused the room numbers until he located the one he knew belonged to her. Knocking abruptly, he waited impatiently for her to answer the door, glancing at his watch when she didn't appear right away.

She wasn't there.

Neil's eyes narrowed, his mood grim. If she wasn't in her hotel room and she wasn't with him, then where precisely—

The sound of familiar feminine laughter struck his ears and made its way down his spine. Neil turned around slowly, cautiously, all of his senses on alert. Eyes narrowing in possessiveness, his hands balled into fists as he watched Valentina's voluptuous form leave a suite that didn't belong to her. Giggling, her eyes went wide in— shock? fright?—as she came to a halt in front of him.

"Neil," she breathed out, "what are you doing here?"

His eyes flicked over her breasts before settling on her face. "I think," he said distinctly, his words clipped, "that the more appropriate question is where in the bloody hell have you been and who have you been with?"

Valentina's eyes rounded. She'd just come back from helping Cynthia settle in across the hall so she hadn't been able to go to him today as she'd planned. And yesterday— she sighed—yesterday she had been so distraught over the idea of leaving Scotland, of leaving Neil, that she hadn't been able to work up a sexual appetite of any sort whatsoever. Seduction had been the last thing on her mind at the time.

She supposed she'd better lay all of her cards on the table and tell him her feelings. After all, there were only six more days left. "I think we better go inside my suite and talk."

His nostrils flared. "Like bloody hell."

Valentina spun on her heel, thinking Neil was about to leave her, her heart plummeting because of that fact. But he didn't walk all the way back to the elevators. Instead of leaving her forever, as she thought he was about to do, he stopped in front of Cynthia's suite and started pounding on the door like a man possessed.

"Open up, you goddamned bastard!"

Valentina's jaw went slack as it dawned on her that Neil thought she'd been inside of Cynthia's hotel room with another man. If she hadn't been so elated by the fact that he was jealous, that he didn't want her with anybody else, she would have thrown something at him to keep him from humiliating her in front of her best friend. He was banging on the door quite loudly after all.

"Neil," Valentina said, her voice finally working as she rushed over to his side, "please quit pounding on that door. You're going to regret it!"

"Oh I am, am I?" he said through clenched teeth, the veins and muscles in his forearms visibly cording. "Somehow I doubt that." He pounded louder, his voice gone mad. "Open up damn it! Open up this door before I kick it...uhhhh...in," he finished softly.

Neil stared down at the tiny form of a very beautiful African-American...*woman*. He was so taken aback by his mistake, so grateful that it indeed had been a mistake, that all he could do was continue staring down at her.

Cynthia's hands flew to her hips. She scowled up at him. "The door is open, Rambo. Now what can I do for you?"

Valentina was quick to intercept. "Cynthia," she said, clearing her throat, "I'd like for you to meet Neil. Neil, this is my best friend, Cynthia."

"Cynthia," Neil repeated, his dark eyes lighting up, his lips kicking into a grin. He was simply too relieved to be embarrassed. "How do you do?"

She shook his hand and chuckled, effectively letting him off the hook. "I'm doing all right considering I almost got my ass whooped for having an affair with my best friend."

Neil had the good grace to look chagrined at that. "I, uh, I had no intention of whooping your ass as you so plainly put it. I was just, uh—I was extremely anxious to make your acquaintance."

"Uh-huh."

"It's true. Tina's told me a great deal about you."

"Uh-huh." Cynthia grinned. "The doors aren't soundproof you know. I heard everything you said to Tina before you threatened to kick in the door."

Valentina bit her lip, stifling a grin. She was pleased to note that Neil was recovering quickly.

"Well," he burred, "perhaps you will allow me the privilege of making this rather awkward meeting up to you tomorrow. Perhaps I can take the two of you out for drinks or something?"

Cynthia chuckled, nodding her acceptance. "Sounds good." Her eyes flicked toward Valentina. "You two go ahead and talk. I've got some phone calls to make." She smiled up to Neil. "Nice meeting you, Rambo. Tina, I'll see you at breakfast."

Valentina chuckled as she watched Cynthia make her way back into her suite. She shook her head at Neil and grinned. "I told you you'd regret it," she murmured.

His smile was sheepish. "I suppose you did."

She waved a hand toward her own suite. "Would you care to come in?"

He met her gaze. "Very much."

A few minutes later, they were seated at a table inside of her suite sharing a bottle of wine. Valentina wasn't certain how she should go about telling him her feelings, but she intuitively sensed that this was the time to make them known. "Neil," she expelled on a sigh of resignation, "we really need to talk."

Neil watched her face, not certain he cared for the expression writ on it. She looked down in the dumps, depressed, perhaps already contemplating her planned departure—a departure he'd do anything to keep her from making. "Go on."

She sighed, smoothing back a tendril of golden brown hair. She met his gaze. "There's something I've been needing to say to you for days now, only I haven't been able to work up the nerve to say it. I..." She took a deep breath and expelled it, looking away.

His stomach knotted. "Is this bad news?" he asked. "Because if it is, I'm not certain I want to hear it. Let me rephrase that. I *know* that I don't want to hear it."

Valentina's smile was bemused. "I suppose the definition of 'bad' depends upon your vantage point." She bit down on her lip and nibbled at it for a moment. "And if I knew what your vantage point was it would be a hell of a lot easier to say what needs to be said."

Neil's eyes raked over her body, over her face. He didn't want to hear any more, didn't want to chance the fact that it could be bad news. In that moment, his only concern was to bind her to him, to keep her with him always. Despite the doubts, the worries he'd sometimes entertained since meeting her, he had always known that when they were together sexually they were as one mind in all things. He decided to use that knowledge to his advantage.

"Come here," he murmured, holding out his hand, "I want to play with you."

Valentina's head shot up. A part of her wanted to say no, to insist that they talk without sexual contact of any sort, but another part of her, the insecure part, wanted to be with him one last time before being forced to tell him that she was in love with him. If he didn't return her feelings after all, she would never be able to be with him again and enjoy it.

And so she stood up and pulled her cotton sundress over her head, exposing herself to him with a few small tugs. She was naked, he was clothed, and for the first time since she'd met him she felt utterly and completely vulnerable to him.

"Come here," he coaxed, his eyes burning into her flesh, "whatever you have to say can be said whilst sitting on my lap."

Valentina walked the small distance that separated them and stood before Neil. Before she could sit down on his lap as he'd told her to, he buried his face against her chest and popped a nipple into his mouth. He drew on it, hardening and elongating it, inducing her eyes to close and her head to fall back on a moan.

Neil's hands roamed all over her body, settling at her tanned buttocks where he palmed and kneaded them as he continued to draw from her breast. He was losing control as he always did when he held her sexually, all higher level thinking quickly discarding itself to be replaced by primitive need. He pushed her hand down to cover his erection and groaned when she began to rub him through the jeans material.

"Take him out and sit on him," he said thickly, releasing her nipple. "I need to feel you wrapped around me."

Valentina did as she'd been bade, unzipping his jeans and freeing his stiff erection. Neil took the liberty of divesting himself of his shirt while she ran her hands over the expanse of his chest, loving the hardness and musculature of it.

"Do you still think we're not suited for each other?" she asked boldly as she came down on him and straddled his lap, her vagina poised at the head of his cock.

Neil's fingers dug into her hips as he surged upwards, groaning as he entered her, gritting his teeth at the feel of her warm, wet flesh enveloping him, taking all of him in. "I never thought…" It was so difficult to speak, so difficult to think. He surged upwards again, wringing a gasp out of her. "I never thought that."

"Then why did you wait until tonight to come to me?" Valentina held herself still, refusing to ride him into orgasm until he answered her. She knew she was toying with him, knew he'd only be able to endure so much.

"Because," he said, his eyes narrowed, the primitive part of his brain fully registering the fact that his sexual mate was withholding from him. His fingers dug deeper into her hips as he thrust upwards in a powerful, smooth motion both of them found highly stimulating. "Because," he ground out, "I wanted to be certain you wanted me here." He surged up again, earning himself another feminine gasp. "But I've decided that I'm keeping you regardless."

Valentina smiled slowly. She rewarded his unexpected answer with some brisk, hard riding. He moaned, his tongue coming out to instinctively curl around her nipple, drawing it in, rolling it around with his lips and tongue.

"I love you, Neil Macalister," she whispered as she rode him, her bald flesh sucking up his cock over and over again, the sticky sound of their flesh joining echoing in the room. "I love you so much."

There were few things that could have penetrated Neil's brain in the midst of being in full rut, but those words were at the top of the list. His dark eyes widened as he released her nipple and gazed into her light green eyes. "Then marry me, Tina, because I love you too, darlin'."

Valentina smiled fully, bending forward to kiss him on the lips. "I was beginning to think you'd never ask."

"I don't want you to go back to Atlanta," he said in a dominant brogue, his eyes searching hers. "Not now, not ever."

"I know. I'm not."

He grunted arrogantly. There was only so much intelligent conversation a highly erect man could engage in at one sitting. Especially when said man was buried to the hilt inside the woman of his dreams.

In one fluid motion he stood up, his arms wrapped around her, their bodies still joined, and carried her over to the bed. Coming down on top of her, he paused in his lovemaking long enough to growl out one last command. "No more birth control pills."

"You want me to have your baby?" she whispered.

He merely grunted in response.

Valentina giggled, taking that as a yes. She splayed her thighs wide, giving him ready access to the flesh he needed. Neil surged in deeply, groaning as he re-entered her, and rode them both into mindless oblivion.

Epilogue
Five Years Later

Neil stood atop the mountain of Cairn Gorm in the purplish early morning light, reflecting on what a glorious life he was leading. Five years of marriage to the woman he loved, successful careers for both of them, two gorgeous daughters, and now Valentina told him they were expecting their third child to make an appearance into the world sometime around Christmas.

Life had been decidedly good to them, had blessed them, and thankfully showed every sign of continuing to do so. Even their friends had found good luck, Valentina's best friend Cynthia and Neil's best friend John having fallen in love and married only weeks after meeting. Cynthia had retained custody of Erica, she and John had created another child together, and their family of four's posh flat was but a five minute walk from the Macalisters'.

Neil's gaze strayed from the view below the mountain back over to where the nude body of his sleeping wife lay. He smiled slowly, thinking to himself that life was full of poignant ironies. If someone had told him a week or even a day before he'd met Valentina that five years later he would be standing naked atop a mountain in the Highlands celebrating his fifth wedding anniversary to the most provocative woman he'd ever laid eyes upon, he would have told them they were insane. But that was indeed what had happened.

Neil walked back to where his wife was asleep and kneeled down beside her. His dark eyes crinkled at the corners as she slowly came awake and reached out for him, wanting him to become a part of her.

He came down on top of her, burying himself in her warmth, knowing a day would never go by when he wouldn't thank the fates for bringing him Valentina.

Neil was, after all, a most sensible man.

VANISHED

To David, for infinite inspiration…

Chapter 1

She'd give anything for some coffee. An oversized mug filled to the rim with the richest, hottest, blackest Columbian elixir ever to grace a coffee cup would have felt like a gift from the gods right about now. But at this point, she thought grimly, even a half-filled Dixie cup that tasted more like water than beans would be enough to make her do a cartwheel.

Lynne Temple sighed as her red SUV idled up yet another twisting, snowy mountain road. She'd been following this temporary route for over an hour now and was beginning to worry that someone had neglected to put up a very necessary sign that would have kept her from heading in the wrong direction.

A semi had jackknifed on the turnpike an hour or so before she'd gotten to it, making the lanes impassable. The police quickly threw up a temporary detour route through the rocky terrain, diverting traffic through a small coalmining town in the remote wilds of West Virginia. Not that there was much traffic in need of being diverted at eleven o'clock on a Tuesday night in a sparsely populated, rural area. Indeed, Lynne had yet to run into another pair of headlights.

For the first time since this little excursion off the beaten path began, a sense of alarm was beginning to settle in. It was pitch-black outside, nothing but the SUV's high beams to break the bleak darkness. The further she drove through the steep terrain, the thicker the wintry forests on either side of the tiny road grew. It was creepy out here, she thought, the tiny hairs at the nape of her neck stirring. Dark, remote, and creepy.

She didn't belong in this place, she knew. Lynne felt—and was—out of her element. To a city girl from the flatlands of Clearwater, Florida, even something as simple as driving on the turnpike set her nerves on edge. The snowy mountains the turnpike cut through were steeper than she'd ever seen. The winds this high up in altitude were harsh during the winter months, beating against the SUV and making her feel as though she would be blown off the side of a cliff at any given moment. She felt no more protected from the elements than she would have felt driving a tin can with four glued-on wheels.

The turnpike had been bad enough. Driving through the bizarre little twisting road nestled somewhere up in the Appalachians was a thousand times worse.

Lynne took a deep breath and exhaled slowly, telling herself not to freak out. So it was dark outside. So the wind was moaning like a demon out of a B-movie. So the gravel road had turned to mud and slush about fifteen minutes ago…

"Great," she muttered under her breath. "This is just great."

She realized that she needed to turn around and follow the winding path back to some manner of civilization, but there wasn't precisely anywhere to turn around. She could stop in the middle of the "road", she supposed, and try to turn around that way, but with her luck she'd finally spot another vehicle while attempting the feat—as it slammed into the side of her new vehicle from out of nowhere.

At first she had assumed she was following the detour correctly, but she couldn't recall the last time she'd seen a sign. Worse yet, she'd made more than a few turns in the past hour and now wasn't altogether certain she could find her way back in the middle of the night. Especially when she considered that the snowfall had been light but steady, so the SUV's tracks were probably already covered up.

What an ironic way to start her new life, Lynne considered, frowning. Thirty-four was supposed to be the year she made life happen instead of waiting for it to come to her. She could design databases from anywhere, but since her largest client was located in the capitol city of Charleston, West Virginia, she'd decided to make the move after the divorce from Steve and settle into a lazy southern house down on the river that saw all four seasons.

It sounded almost idyllic compared to the humid, forever hot beach apartment crammed full of bad memories she'd vacated all of a day ago. And it could still be idyllic—if only she could find her way back to the beaten path.

Lynne's gaze absently flicked toward the fuel tank gage. Her heart rate sped up when she saw that she was down to an eighth of a tank of gas. *Great! This is just damn great.* She blew out a breath, that sense of alarm growing by leaps and bounds.

It was pitch-black outside, the winds were moaning something fierce, she was driving up a muddy, slushy path that led only God knows where, the snowfall was picking up a bit, and now the SUV was running on fumes. She would have laughed if only she weren't so terrified.

Clutching the steering wheel so tightly her knuckles turned white, Lynne's dark brown eyes widened as the narrow path she was traveling up became impossibly narrower. "Shit," she mumbled, deciding it was way past time to turn around. The snowcapped forest to either side of the tiny road was growing thicker…and somehow a lot more intimidating.

Her teeth sank into her lower lip; perspiration broke out on her forehead. She absently tucked a rogue strand of dark brown hair behind an ear as her inner musings turned ugly. As ridiculous as it sounded even to herself, she was afraid to stop the SUV long enough to turn it around. Stopping equaled vulnerability, leaving her naked to outside attack, even if the stop would only last a few seconds.

Lynne blew out a breath, rolling her eyes at her dramatic thoughts. "You've watched one too many horror movies, kiddo," she whispered as she let up on the gas pedal and slowly worked the brake. She hadn't seen another vehicle let alone another person for miles—well over an hour ago by now. The chances of some psycho on the loose nabbing her while she did an about-face in a locked vehicle of all things was about nil to none.

The SUV came to a stop, the lack of movement underscoring the sound of the moaning Appalachian winter wind outside the barricade of the windows. She told herself to ignore it, to forget about the fact she was alone in the middle of a mountaintop forest in the dead of night, and to concentrate on getting the hell out of there.

Backing up enough to turn the vehicle around, she gasped when a movement of some sort snagged her peripheral vision. Her breathing immediately stilled. She blinked and did a double take.

"Damn, damn, damn," she murmured as she kept turning the SUV around. She prayed she was imagining things because she hadn't seen anyone or anything upon second glance. *Just get out of here!* she told herself as the vehicle straightened and she stepped on the accelerator. *Now!*

Flooring it, Lynne's heart rate went over the top as she slammed down on the gas pedal. Probably not the swiftest reflex she'd ever had, for the SUV immediately went into a skid. Mingled mud and ice-slush flew up from all sides, pelting the windshield and making her heart thump like a rock in her chest.

Another movement to the left...

Lynne barely had time to register that she'd seen something when the shadow of a large man appeared from seemingly out of nowhere. She screamed as she slammed down on the brakes and veered a quick right to avoid hitting him, then screamed again when she momentarily lost control of the SUV and it went into a flat spin.

Shaking like a leaf, she tried to recover from the spin, but it was too late. Her eyes widened as the vehicle skidded off the narrow path and headed straight for the trunk of a thick oak tree. Unable to do anything besides go numb from shock, she watched in helpless horror as her brand new cherry red vehicle collided with a mighty oak, smashing the entire front end and simultaneously jarring her body. Frantic, she turned her head to the left to see if that man was still around—or if she'd imagined him altogether.

The automatic airbag in the steering column engaged and a second later she was struck in the side of the head with a life-saving device that damn near killed her. She gasped as the airbag assaulted her, her dark eyes rolling back into her head.

Please don't let me pass out, she thought in terror as the shadow of a very real, and very large, man emerged from the forest. *Oh God—oh please—I must have sustained a concussion...*

Lynne's vision began to dim at the precise moment the stranger's form appeared in her remaining headlight and began to steadily walk toward her SUV. He was huge—at least a foot taller than her own five feet—and was wearing a one-piece jumper of some sort. His face was grim, his sharp gaze intense.

As her eyes slowly began to close, she considered the possibility that maybe the stranger was a mechanic. Mechanics tended to wear those blue issue one-piece jumpsuits. Maybe he could even help fix the SUV.

Her dulling gaze flicked toward the stranger's vein-roped hands. Hysteria bubbled up inside of her when she saw that his hands were chained together. And, she thought, ice-cold horror lancing through her, so were his ankles…

Lynne's heart violently pumped away in her chest even as she slipped into the black void of unconsciousness. He was an escaped convict, her mind screamed, the reality that she was about to pass out unavoidable. Oh God—

Oh please, she thought as her eyes irrevocably closed, *please somebody help me!*

Chapter 2

Lynne softly moaned as she tried to open her heavy eyelids. Her face scrunched up when a dull, thumping pain lanced through the right side of her brain. She groaned, her hand instinctively flying up to cover the injured area.

The events she'd undergone prior to the pain registering were slowly creeping back into her consciousness. Divorcing Steve after he'd slept with various other women, picking up and moving to Charleston, the detour on the turnpike, the fear she'd felt at being out in the middle of nowhere alone…

The skidding SUV. Colliding with a tree. The airbag engaging—

The stranger.

She stilled. The stranger. The big man wearing what she now understood to be a prison-issued jumpsuit.

Oh damn—where was he now? Was he here? Had he taken her somewhere? Or was she still in the SUV, left out in the middle of a mountain winterscape with a totaled vehicle and internal injuries to fend for herself? As her belly clenched and knotted, she profusely hoped it was the latter. She had a cell phone, she recalled. Somewhere in her brand new smashed up baby there was a way to call for help.

Lynne tried once more to open her eyes, a strange nearby sound inducing her forehead to wrinkle. The steady noise was foreign, yet eerily familiar. She couldn't place it, but realized she should have been able to.

Trees. For some reason the grating sound brought to mind trees. But what about them? Trees being chopped down maybe? No, she thought, that wasn't quite right. Trees being—

Trees being sawed down. That's what it brought to mind. Trees being sawed down...

Her breathing stilled.

A saw—what she heard was a saw.

She swallowed heavily, able to venture an accurate guess that it most likely wasn't a tree currently being sawed through. Most likely it was metal, metal from two sets of shackles she remembered with crisp, dawning awareness.

Oh God, Lynne thought, her heart beating like mad in her chest, *I've got to open my eyes and get out of here. Out of here before those shackles are completely gone and I don't stand a chance of outrunning him!*

"I was wondering when you'd wake up," a masculine voice murmured. The sound of metal clinging against a wood floor instantly dashed all hopes of outrunning him. The shackles were off. "Might as well open your eyes. I know you're awake."

The knot in her belly tightened. Her breasts heaved up and down with her labored breathing. She didn't want to open her eyes. Oh goodness, seeing the owner of the low but commanding voice would make this nightmare just a bit too real.

But it is real. It's real and you better deal with it. Figure out a way to escape him, Lynne. For once in your thirty-four pathetic years, use your damn brain!

Unfortunately her brain and her nervous system were feeling the affects of too much reality. Reality was that she had been kidnapped—there was no way a convict on the run would ever let her just up and go. Reality also dictated that the stranger hadn't been imprisoned for a menial crime like a traffic violation. No one would bother to escape from prison if their offense was minor and they were due to get paroled in a few months.

Her breathing grew more labored as she considered the possibilities. She could only hope it was a white-collar crime, even if it was a serious one. The idea of being kidnapped by an embezzler was much more palatable than the many other scenarios pounding through her mind.

Arson. Drug trafficking. Murder...

The sound of approaching footsteps made her gasp. Her dark brown eyes flew open and clashed with very intense, and horrifically familiar, green ones. She stilled.

"Oh my God," Lynne breathed out, her eyes round as full moons. She knew that face—even covered in stubble as it now was. Everyone in Florida knew that face. The entire state had seen it plastered all over the news. But what was a wanted fugitive who was known for stalking his prey along the Florida/Georgia border doing here, miles and miles away in West Virginia?

The stranger looming over her, the one looking more ominous by the moment, was no stranger at all. Not exactly. She recognized him all right. She even knew his name.

"You're Jesse Redshaw," she whispered, her voice catching in the back of her throat. She gulped, realizing as soon as the words came tumbling out that she would have been wiser to pretend she had no idea who he was.

Those intense, grim eyes of his grazed over her face, then down lower to her heaving chest. Suddenly she remembered what it was he'd been convicted of, why he was a wanted man. It wasn't because of embezzling, or drug trafficking, or even murder—all of which seemed like more ideal crimes at the moment.

The huge, muscled man who now held all power over her was what the police in Florida called a sexual predator, Lynne thought in terror, feeling as if she might pass out for a second time. He was a sadistic, serial rapist...

His light brown head came up slowly. A jagged scar that zigzagged across the left side of his jaw became visible. That scar of his was basically what had ended up convicting him in the first place. Not too many men could claim to have a similar one. It resembled an imperfect lightning bolt.

The crew cut his hair was fashioned in gave him a rigid, merciless appearance. The snake tattoo that wound up his vein-roped arm added more menace to the overall picture. He was tall, heavily muscled, and stern-looking.

His unfathomable green gaze raked over her breasts again before sweeping back up to her face.

Oh God, Lynne thought, her breathing so heavy she just knew she was close to passing out. Her worst nightmare had come chillingly true. She'd been kidnapped, had no doubt vanished without a trace to the outside world. She would never leave here untouched, perhaps not even alive.

Jesse Redshaw was a serial rapist who stood a foot taller and probably a hundred and fifty pounds heavier than Lynne. He was a serial rapist who hadn't been able to touch a woman in five plus years—not until now, not until he'd escaped...

Lynne's horrified gaze clashed with his frightening one. She recalled the most recent news report she'd seen on him, the one that claimed his last two victims had been found brutally stabbed and left for dead.

He was a murderer, too. A rapist and a murderer. The irony that she was going to die because someone had neglected to post accurate detour signs was not lost on her.

"What are you going to do with me?" she whispered.

Chapter 3

One of his eyebrows slowly inched up as he intently regarded her face. "I haven't decided," he murmured. "I'll let you know when I do." He turned on his heel and walked to the other side of what she now realized to be a log cabin of sorts.

Lynne briefly closed her eyes, long enough to take a deep breath in an effort to keep from passing out again. Jesse Redshaw, she thought, bile creeping its way up her throat. Back in Florida he was more infamous than Ted Bundy, considered to be more ruthless too. Ted Bundy, a man who had been executed by the state in the electric chair years ago, had supposedly knocked his victims out quickly, waiting until they were dead before doing grisly things to them. According to rumor, Jesse Redshaw did those things while his prey was still alive...and cognizant of what was being done to them.

The adrenaline rush she'd initially experienced upon first recognition plummeted, leaving her numb and chilled to the bone. Her teeth began to chatter as she glanced around the cabin, noting every possible escape route. There was only one...the front door. Somehow that knowledge made her feel even more hopeless, more sunken and depressed.

The log cabin was small—very small. It was composed of only one room sectioned off into three distinct areas. Closest to the fireplace was the bedroom, which amounted to the bed she'd been laid out on plus a small knotty pine dresser. On the "far" side of the cabin, where Jesse Redshaw now stood, was the kitchen. It consisted of a miniature stove, a sink, a small, knotted pine table, and two cupboards. And, finally, the bathroom lay in the middle. It boasted nothing more than a toilet.

Sweet lord above, she couldn't die here, she told herself, her teeth chattering away like mad. Not here. Please not here…

Lynne bolted upright in the bed, the goose down covers she'd been swaddled in pooling around her waist. Her breasts were revealed to the chilled room, her dark rose nipples stabbing out from the cold. She gasped at the realization that she was naked, then gasped again as pain shot through her skull. She cried out as she fell backward onto the bed, the throbbing in her head too unbearable to even consider the possible ramifications inherent in the fact that her naked breasts were on display.

"Quit thrashing around," a masculine voice growled in low tones. She felt the bed dip slightly and knew he had seated himself next to her on it. "Your head took a real beating from the airbag. It must have caused something in the SUV to gash your head, too. Jarring it around like that ain't helping."

Lynne couldn't have opened her eyes if her life depended on it. Her entire face was scrunched up into a frozen mask of pain, the endless pounding in her head like a migraine amplified a thousand times over. "H-Hurts," she gasped, clutching her head. "H-Help—hurts."

"Shh now, calm down. You're working yourself up," he softly drawled, his southern accent detectable.

She was worked up for many reasons. Pain was only one of them. Wondering how much more pain she would be dealt, only the next time at the gigantic man's hands, was the major one. Fortunately, the current pain she was experiencing was far too intense to be able to dwell on any of the heinous possibilities.

He grabbed her hand and forcibly lowered it from the injury. Jesse Redshaw, she thought—Jesse Redshaw! This was like waking up to find Hannibal Lecter leaning over you with a carving knife and a bottle of Chianti.

"If you keep touching it, I'll have to tie you down," he murmured, making her body still for the first time. "I've gone through a lot of trouble to get this wound healed up—five days worth of trouble as a matter of fact—and I won't see you undo the results."

Lynne hysterically wondered if he was healing her up just so he could have the fun of slicing her back apart, but wisely, she held her tongue. "I'm sorry," she whispered, her eyelids briefly fluttering open. She tried to focus on his face, but couldn't. The pain had blurred her vision. All she could register were those piercing green eyes of his staring down at her. "Sorry," she muttered, her eyes closing again.

"Just keep your eyes shut," he said in a quiet rumble. "I'm going to try and get some more soup down you after you rest up a bit."

His words sparked some distant memory in Lynne—a flashback to the five days she'd spent unconscious perhaps? Small impressions, threadbare flickers of awareness:

Strong hands holding her up. Warm beef broth running down her throat. The feel of a cool rag pressing against her head followed by the pungent scent of ointment. Hot breath whispering soothing words into her ear. A rough tongue curling around one of her stiff nipples...

Lynne silently whimpered as she quickly plummeted toward inevitable slumber. She hoped she had imagined the last bit, and that Jesse Redshaw held no interest in her as a woman, or more importantly, as potential prey. She could have sworn he liked blondes. Then again, maybe the five years long dry spell of victims had made him less choosy. She prayed that wasn't the case.

"Go to sleep," her captor murmured, his large hands falling to the covers pooled below her navel. He slowly drew them up her body, the calluses on his fingers making goose bumps form where they raked across bared skin. "And by the way, I prefer brunettes."

Lynne would have gasped if she'd had the energy, but since she didn't, mentally cringing would have to suffice. She hadn't intended to say those words about his past victims aloud — only to think them.

The last flicker of awareness she entertained before drifting off into a deep, lulling sleep was the impression of covers being swaddled around her body to warm her...

And the pad of a thumb grazing over one jutting nipple before the covers were raised to her neck.

* * * * *

When Lynne next awoke, it was to the feel of warm broth drizzling down her throat. Her eyelids tentatively fluttered, batting away at the grogginess.

He was still here, she thought, her eyes opening. Jesse Redshaw was very real and very much here.

Lynne's gaze clashed with his. Her heart began thumping in her chest. He said nothing in response to her anxiety, just held her stare for a moment before glancing back down to her mouth and continued to feed her.

The next twenty minutes were spent like this. No words. No frights. Nothing alarming. Just the captor feeding liquid to his captive like a helpless baby bird, and the captive warily studying the grim features of the man who had, for reasons unknown, saved her life.

It was hard to credit. It was difficult to take in the fact that a man for whom killing and torturing was his chief *raison d' etre* in life was showing her such incredible kindness and gentleness. At least for now.

Her dark gaze nervously flicked along his face, over the scar marring his chin, then down lower to his hands and vein-roped arms. He was a strong man—very strong and heavily muscled, she thought, staring at the snake tattoo winding up his arm. But then he would have to be strong to make it this long without getting recaptured by the authorities. Especially considering the fact that he had been shackled clear up until she'd awoken the last time…however long ago that was.

Jesse Redshaw had managed to escape from custody, trek all the way from Stark, Florida near the Georgia border to West Virginia, carry Lynne's body to wherever they were currently holed up at, feed and care for her injuries—all while shackled. That required more inhuman patience, perseverance, cunning, and strength than she was comfortable crediting him with.

Lynne kept her mouth open, the warm liquid feeling good running down her raw throat as her gaze crept back up to his face. She recalled reading a true crime novel some years back that stated how average-looking the run-of-the-mill sexual offender was. He tended to be completely nondescript, sometimes even handsome, not at all possessing the monstrous appearance one would expect.

That had been true of Ted Bundy. Ted Bundy had been dashingly handsome with soulful eyes and an ornery grin. Jesse Redshaw was even more striking in a ruggedly masculine way. Lynne couldn't help but wonder exactly where it had all gone wrong. Had her captor been sadistic since childhood? Had he been born evil or had he become it?

She also found herself wondering how old he was, unable to recall that particular bit of information. She could have sworn the news said he was forty, but he looked more like thirty-five. Then again, the crinkles at the corners of his eyes bespoke of maturity.

Not that it really mattered. Whether thirty-five or forty, Jesse Redshaw was still in control of the situation. And her. For now.

"How are you feeling?" he rumbled out, his gaze finding hers.

She swallowed. "Better," she whispered. Her eyes widened a bit. "Where are we? How many days have gone by?"

He stood, the bedsprings creaking at the loss of weight. "A week," he informed her as he strode to the other side of the cabin toward the kitchen. The muscles in his back rippled against the semi-tight jumpsuit he wore. "The first time you woke it had been five days. You slept another two."

A week.

Lynne bit down hard on her lower lip as her stomach muscles clenched. Surely her mom would have reported her missing six days ago, yet she still hadn't been rescued. Maybe she would never be rescued. If the police were smart they'd look for her in the area where the turnpike detour had been thrown up. Then again, she drove approximately an hour away from that temporary route before crashing into the oak tree. And lord only knows where she was now. Her captor had yet to answer that question. Somehow, she nervously conceded, she doubted that he ever would.

"I was wondering…"

He cocked his head and stared at her from over his shoulder. His light brown hair had grown a bit longer since she'd last awoken. Not much, but a little. The crew cut looked a bit thicker. His face was still as grim and impassive as ever, though. A realization that made her heartbeat quicken from anxiety.

Lynne's mouth worked up and down, but nothing came out. She was trying her damnedest to calm herself, but it wasn't working. "I—I..."

"Yes?"

He seemed a bit impatient now. Or angry. Dear God, the last thing she wanted to do was make him angry. Firmly tampering down on her raw fear, she blithered out her question before her courage to ask it once again deserted her. "Have you decided what you are going to do with me?"

Her captor stilled from where he stood at the tiny sink. He stared at her for a long moment, his gaze raking over her, before turning to stare out the small window before him. "Yes," he softly drawled, "I have."

Oh damn, she thought, her breathing growing labored. She almost wished she hadn't asked. This was it. The moment her last seven days of recovery came down to. His final decision. "Will you tell me what it is?" she whispered.

Lynne's eyes slowly widened as Jesse Redshaw began peeling off his jumpsuit. Her adrenaline started pumping like a broken dam, worsening with every inch of bare skin and hard muscle revealed to her. First his back—a wide, chiseled back tattooed with Celtic tribal markings. Then his arms—strong, vein-roped arms that looked like they could effortlessly kill her. Then his boxer shorts—cotton and no doubt prison-issued.

Perspiration broke out on her forehead as she watched her captor step out of the jumpsuit until all he wore were those white boxers. His legs were as powerful as the rest of him, she hysterically noted.

"I've decided to keep you," he murmured, his back still to her. He paused a suspenseful moment, then turned around slowly. "For now."

Her breathing ragged, she flew up into a sitting position, heedless of her bared breasts. He was going to rape her, she realized, her eyes wide with terror. Rape her and then kill her when he got bored with her.

"I want to live," she breathed out, her chest dramatically heaving, her nipples tight now from excessive adrenaline instead of cold.

His eyebrows shot up. He opened his mouth to speak, but whatever he was about to say was forgotten when he noticed her breasts. His eyes grew immediately heavy-lidded, his penis beginning to swell against the boxers.

Lynne went with that. She was hysterical. Half out of her mind with fear and frenzy. It was easy to imagine how heroic one would behave if the situation wasn't happening to them—a different ballgame entirely when it actually was. "I—I'll do anything you say," she pleaded. "Please—I…I know I can make you happy," she said shakily.

She forced a nervous smile to her lips, threw the covers totally off of her, and spread her legs wide open for him as she turned her body to face him. Her heart was thumping so hard she felt ready to pass out yet again. She took comfort in the knowledge that he was growing very erect as he stared at her exposed labia.

Her greatest hope was that he preferred his prey alive. She needed to stall him. Somehow she would get away before he killed her, she fervently vowed to herself.

"You see," she said quietly, nervously. "I—I won't r-resist."

He frowned at her. His jaw clenched. "Look, lady—"

"Oh please!" Lynne cried out as she shot up to her feet. The action made her dizzy, a bit nauseous, but she quickly recovered. She had no idea what she'd done wrong, but conceded that the mind of a sociopath wasn't exactly normal. She needed to make him see things her way, she hysterically thought.

Not knowing what else to do, she fell down onto her knees before him, frantically pulled down his boxing shorts, and wrapped her hands around his long, thick penis. "I can learn to please you," she breathed out. "If you'd give me a chance—" She stopped chattering long enough to swipe her tongue across the head of his cock. He hissed, his stomach muscles clenching. A good sign, she frenetically assured herself. "I can try to keep you very happy," she shakily reiterated.

"Listen," her captor growled. "I will decide—"

She took his tight balls into her mouth, hoping the sound of his breath sucking in meant something good. Lynne sucked on them like her life depended upon it, which it no doubt did, as her hands pumped his huge shaft up and down.

"Shit," he hoarsely muttered.

His breathing was labored, she realized. He liked the way she was sucking his balls and masturbating him. Hope surged inside of her as she released his balls and took his cock into her mouth without missing a beat. She immediately deep-throated him, sucking him off by taking him all the way in and out, over and over, again and again.

He began to moan. His fingers wound through her hair. Hope increased in leaps and bounds.

"Faster," he said thickly.

Lynne sucked faster. She sucked like there was no tomorrow, her every thought to please him. Her head frenziedly bobbed back and forth as she repeatedly deep-throated him. His fingers tightened in her long, dark hair as he moaned and groaned and growled.

When her jaw began to ache she ignored it. She took him deeper into her throat instead, sucking on his cock faster and harder. She had to forget the pain. She had to prove to him that she put his wants first. It was the only way to gain his trust, she reasoned. It was the only way to stall for time.

"Just like that," her captor gritted out. He palmed either side of her face with callused fingers and threw his hips at her, screwing her mouth. He groaned long and loud as he pumped her face. "Fuck—oh shit—I'm coming."

The sudden tensing of his entire body underlined his words. He grabbed the back of her head as his cock plunged in and out from between her suctioning lips. He came on a loud growl, his body shuddering as he spurted warm cum into her mouth.

Lynne drank all of it up, careful not to leave even one salty drop. She had no idea if refusing his cum would set him off, so the thought of not swallowing never once crossed her mind.

Even when he'd been depleted of cum and his labored breathing began to steady, she still didn't quit sucking from the tiny hole at the head of his cock. She waited until he nudged her face away from him to stop, then watched through wide brown eyes as he pulled her up to her feet to face him.

"I need some sleep," he said between ragged breaths. His grim, unsmiling face took on an even harsher quality than normal. "I haven't slept in days," he rasped.

Lynne wasn't certain how to respond. "Then go to sleep," she nervously whispered. She cleared her throat. "I won't try to run."

Jesse stared down at her for a suspended moment, his breathing growing more and more normal. "I'm real sorry to have to do this, but I can't trust—"

"Oh please don't," Lynne breathed out. She realized in hysterical horror that nothing good could possibly follow a sentence like that. "I—oh goodness, I promise I won't try to run! I promise!"

"I know you won't," he replied in a firm tone as he took her by the hand and led her toward the bed. "Because I'll make sure you won't."

Bile began to creep its way up Lynne's throat. She wanted to cry, but perversely, no tears would come. "Oh please don't, sir—Mr. Redshaw. I—oh please!"

He didn't reply.

By the time they reached the bed her teeth were chattering and her body was shaking. She stared at nothing through unblinking eyes, her mind quickly disassociating from her body. He spoke words but she didn't hear them. Lynne felt nothing. She was lost in surreality, unable to believe this was happening to her.

"I said look at me!" Jesse snapped, shaking her by the arms. "Do you hear me? I said you're okay."

Lynne blinked. The words "you're okay" somehow reeled her back down to earth and sanity...at least a little bit.

"You're okay," he murmured, his tone a bit gentler. His intense green gaze raked over her color-drained face. "I've only collared you is all. So you can't run." He held up a chain, showing what he'd done to her while her mind had been some place far, far away.

Lynne blinked again, recognition dawning. It was a chain, just as he'd said, she thought, somewhat relieved. A chain attached to…

Her hand floated up, touching her neck. Her forehead wrinkled.

A dog collar. Good God, she was naked and wearing a dog collar. A week ago having something like this done to her would have made her bawl like a baby. Today it made her shoulders slump in relief.

"Thank you, Mr. Redshaw," she said quietly, her head bowed. He wasn't the only tired one. These extreme emotions she was continuously put through were exhausting.

"The name's Jesse," he muttered, running a hand over his stubbly jaw. "And I know yours is Lynne because I went through your purse."

Her head came up slowly. She watched as he collapsed onto the bed and sprawled out.

"Come sleep next to me," her captor instructed without opening his eyes. "The collar will keep you from leaving, but I still want you to rest up."

Lynne immediately complied, giving him no reason to become angry with her. As she climbed under the covers next to Jesse Redshaw, her naked buttocks pressed against his equally naked, but flaccid penis, she found herself wondering why he cared about her health at all. In the end, she decided not to question what was presumably her good luck.

As long as she was alive, there was hope.

Chapter 4

Jesse awoke to the feel of his captive's mouth sucking on his stiff cock. He hissed as he came fully awake, his breath catching in the back of his throat as he opened his eyes and watched Lynne's beautiful mouth give him another one of her toe-curling blowjobs. The collar around her neck heightened his arousal, his attraction to images of female submission longstanding and undeniable.

He realized why she was sucking him off, of course. He wasn't stupid or easily fooled.

His captive didn't want to die. She was doing everything she could think of to try and keep him happy with her, satisfied by her. She was doing her damnedest to anticipate his needs before he even had them.

She was damn good at it. He felt lost in arousal, his thinking on par with a horny Neanderthal's. He hadn't been with a woman in a long, long time. So long it seemed like a lifetime ago. It was hard to focus on anything besides Lynne.

"What else do you give besides head?" Jesse murmured, his voice thick. He stared down at her from under heavy eyelids, his cock stiffer than he could ever remember it being. "I bet you have a sweet, tight pussy."

Her dark head immediately came up. Long, shiny, chestnut-colored hair framed an exotically sexy face. Her lips were a bit red and puffy, hinting at what she'd been down there doing. Her cheeks were high, her nose small. But her best features, in his estimation, were her chocolate brown eyes. They were round and full, giving her the look of a naïve little doe.

She wet her lips. "I—it's tight, yes," she whispered. "My vagina, I mean." She cleared her throat. "Would you like to feel it?"

Guilt knotted in Jesse's stomach, inducing a frown to mar his face. Lynne must have thought he was angry with her, for her eyes widened and she quickly shot up, preparing to straddle his lap.

His cock was so stiff it ached. His jaw was clenched, his muscles tight. He wanted inside of her cunt more than he wanted to breathe, but...

"Lynne," he growled. "I—"

"I promise it's tight," she said quickly, that half-hysterical look back in her eyes. "I haven't had sex in a really long time." Her smile was shaky. "If you'd just give me a chance and let me put you inside me, I'm sure you'll think it's tight enough."

Jesse blew out a breath.

"And if you don't," she added in a rush, "uh, well...I can do exercises that will make me tighter." She bounded up on top of him without further ado and took his thick cock in between her small hands. "I promise to make you feel good," she whispered, her eyes nervously searching his face as if waiting for an answer.

All this sweet, sexual compliance made it hard to think rationally. She was straddling his lap, her pussy hole poised at the head of his cock, her gorgeous, full breasts with distended rosy nipples revealed to him. Seeing the collar around her neck, the same one secured to a chain locked to a bolt on the floor, made his erection stiffer by the second.

He wanted to fuck her—badly. So badly his balls ached. The guilt was there, but it couldn't compete.

"Let's see how tight your pussy is," Jesse said thickly. His large hands reached up and palmed her breasts. His thumbs ran over her nipples, elongating them. "Wrap it around my cock."

Lynne immediately obeyed. He gritted his teeth as she sank down onto him, his stiff penis securely enveloped inside of the warmest, tightest, juiciest cunt he'd ever felt. He groaned as she began to slowly ride him, her pussy even more suctioning than her mouth.

She looked like the perfect little slave girl, a mental image he had a hard time not conjuring up given the situation. So sweet and sexy, so submissively docile and eager to cater to the master's whims. He didn't want to see Lynne in that light, for his fetish had brought enough pain to his life already, but he couldn't help it. The desire to sexually dominate the woman who belonged to him was as intrinsic to his character as breathing.

"Faster," he ground out. "You have to work harder than this to please me."

Her eyes widened as she picked up the pace, instantaneously obeying him. His nostrils flared as her gorgeous tits jiggled in his palms. He leaned his head up so he could play with her nipples, flicking and licking them while she bounced up and down on his cock. He wrapped his lips around one of her nipples on a moan, the hard ride she was giving him driving him out of his mind with arousal.

Yesterday, before she'd made him come the first time, Jesse had climbed out of the uniform he'd stolen from a prison janitor simply because the fireplace had made the tiny cabin too hot. It didn't take much to overheat such a small space. He hadn't much thought about how Lynne would react to it until she'd freaked out on him, obviously assuming he meant to rape her then and there.

He had been too exhausted to stand up, let alone force sex on someone. But then she hadn't known that.

Jesse had tried to tell Lynne that he had no intention of killing her. But every time he'd opened his mouth to speak, she had forestalled him. First with frantic words, then with a mind-numbing blowjob. After that he'd been too damn tired to say anything at all, considering he hadn't slept more than an hour at a time while she'd been sick.

When he woke up, she had been sucking him stiff. Again, rational thought had deserted him. And now here he lay, his buxom, naked captive fucking his cock, his lips drawing from one of her long nipples. He was already this close to giving her his cum for a second time.

His head fell back on the bed, his breathing ragged. "Make me come, Lynne," he said hoarsely, his jaw tight. He released her breasts and put his hands behind his head as if preparing to watch a movie. "Put on a show for me. Grind your cunt hard around my cock. Make those gorgeous tits jiggle."

Lynne closed her eyes and followed his instruction to the letter. She rode him faster—harder—bouncing away on top of him at a brisk pace that kept her breasts bobbing up and down in the way he liked.

"I'm getting close," he rasped. "Work for it, Lynne. Earn my cum."

She bit down onto her bottom lip and rode him so fast that even she couldn't help but to softly moan. Jesse supposed she probably didn't want to feel pleasure, which he could understand given her suppositions about what might become of her, but his ego very much needed her to feel it.

"You're so sexy," he murmured. "I love your body." He sucked in his breath as her riding became impossibly more vigorous. "Keep those tits bouncing," he said hoarsely.

221

Lynne whimpered as she fucked him, the friction she was feeling against her clit obvious. He wanted her to fuck him longer, until she couldn't stop herself from orgasming no matter how hard she tried, but he couldn't stave off his need for release a second longer.

Her jiggling tits. The feel and sound of her wet, warm cunt fucking him. Her flushed face. The dog collar around her neck—

Every muscle in Jesse's body corded and tensed as he prepared to come. "Shit," he muttered, his eyes closing. His teeth ground together as he broke on a loud groan, hot sperm shooting out of his cock in what felt like an endless stream of seed. Lynne continued to bounce away on top of him, her luscious cunt extracting all of the cum he had to give.

When he was done, when his balls had been totally depleted, he pulled his captive's body down to cover his as best it could, his mouth unthinkingly seeking out hers for a kiss. In her first act of defiance, Lynne turned her face away, giving him her cheek.

Jesse closed his eyes and sighed, letting it go. Her first act of defiance. And, ironically enough, the only one that wielded the power to hurt him.

* * * * *

Lynne crawled out of bed after her captor fell asleep, her chain allowing her as far as the kitchen. She stood before the tiny kitchen window, her body shaking like a leaf, as she peered out of it and into a void of snow, trees, and nothingness. She had no idea where they were, but conceded that wherever it was, it was well hidden from the rest of the world.

As far as the eye could see, there was only wintry mountaintop forest. No other cabins, no paths suggesting roads, no people, no nothing. She didn't even see any animals scurrying around, though she guessed they were probably out there somewhere.

It's amazing how quickly life can take a U-turn, she thought, sighing. Her hand floated up to her neck where she absently stroked the collar she wore — the collar that made escape all the more difficult if not downright impossible.

A week ago she had set out to begin a new life. She'd gotten one all right, Lynne grimly acknowledged. In spades.

This wasn't supposed to happen, she thought sadly. Life was supposed to be better, not worse, after divorcing Steve. She had given her ex-husband ten years of her life — ten years she could never get back — only to end up a naked prisoner wearing a dog collar and a chain. She was weary and downright sick of being victimized by men.

Lynne had been raised to be a good girl who followed the rules. She had never been particularly social, had always been on the shy side, and had fallen in love with Steve most likely because he was the first man to make an effort at drawing her out of her shell.

She had been a very devoted wife. She'd been loyal, hardworking, and so submissive it made her teeth grit to remember. All that had gotten her was a cheating husband who used her timid nature against her to extract anything he wanted from her. Life at the Temple house had always revolved around Steve, never Lynne.

Turning thirty-four made something inside of Lynne wake up like a sleeping bear that had been hibernating for over three decades. Why thirty-four she didn't know. Most people woke up around thirty or forty. At any rate, she'd filed divorce papers, told Steve to get the hell out of their apartment, and took off for Charleston the day the divorce was finalized.

Life had felt great. Lynne had felt great. Driving down the interstate to a new destiny had awakened hope inside of her she didn't know existed. And then came the crash. And Jesse Redshaw. She sighed.

Lynne didn't know what to make of her captor. Jesse Redshaw was a serial rapist, yes, but according to the news reports he was a sadist, too. Wouldn't a sadist have enjoyed her pain? Wouldn't a sadist have wanted to watch her die, or at least inflict more degradation and suffering into the sexual act after saving her?

She took a deep breath and slowly expelled it. Maybe he was saving that "treat" for later. Perhaps he was savoring their time together, settling for the infliction of mental fright in the short run in order to draw the moment out. But then why would he have spent seven days caring for her, feeding her, and healing her?

Her captor was an enigma. A six-and-some-odd-foot, two-hundred-and-fifty pounds of muscle mystery.

Lynne's stomach growled, underscoring the fact she hadn't eaten anything since yesterday. She opened the two tiny kitchen cupboards and sighed in relief when she saw they were still stocked half full. She hesitated for the briefest moment, wondering if eating without permission would set him off.

In the end, the hunger pangs won out. She rifled through the cupboard doors, deciding to deal with any possible repercussions later.

Lynne needed energy, which meant she needed food. Formulating escape plans was otherwise impossible.

* * * * *

When Jesse woke up later that evening, it was with the intention of setting the record straight with Lynne. He didn't want her worried she was going to die when he knew he couldn't do something like that to her. He doubted she'd believe him, but at least the guilt would quit gnawing at him for having said it.

He'd spent seven days nursing her back to health. The first five days had been the most grueling. Caring for a fevered woman who had suffered trauma to the head took an incredible amount of energy. Doing it while still in prison shackles had downright exhausted him.

But in those days Lynne had spent recuperating, Jesse had come to care for her in a way he wasn't certain he could rationalize. It was the first time another person had ever depended upon him for everything—from feeding them, to dressing their wounds, to bathing them.

She had looked like a helpless little doll, an image further exacerbated by her tiny five-foot frame. The only things that looked womanly and mature about Lynne were her full, ripe breasts and hourglass figure. That looked plenty womanly. And had kept him harder than a tire iron for a solid week.

If he were smart, he wouldn't have brought her here. He would have somehow alerted the police to the fact that an unconscious woman was lying in her vehicle and needed attended to. But the nearest hospital was at least three hours away. Hell, the nearest town, if you could call it that, was over an hour and a half away. Lord only knows how long it would have taken someone to find her—if they ever did. By then she might have died.

The decision to bring Lynne to the cabin nobody knew existed hadn't been difficult. He was her only hope at survival. An irony, others would call it.

Now Lynne was alive and well. And Jesse wanted her to realize he had no desire to change that fact.

When he woke up, he had the best intentions. When he climbed out of bed naked and rock-hard, and saw his nude captive bent over the small kitchen table to clean it, his intentions went to hell in a heartbeat.

Shit, she looked good. Memories seized him. Vivid memories of her tight, hot cunt squeezing his cock until he spurt. Memories of her cushioned thighs straddling his lap, her sexy tits jiggling while she rode him.

"What are you doing?" Jesse murmured.

Lynne froze, her back to him. He knew the question had come out a bit gruff, but that was just how he talked. Something he hoped she got used to real quick.

"I was just cleaning up —" She cleared her throat and spoke a bit louder. "I made some dinner and was cleaning up my mess."

She turned around slowly, her sexy nude body visible to him. He wanted to run his tongue through that tiny patch of black pussy hair. "I left some of the canned stew on the stove for you..." Her voice trailed off and her eyes widened when her gaze flicked down to his hard-on. "Oh," she whispered.

Jesse's eyes raked over her as he walked to where she stood.

"What would you like?" she quietly asked. "Should I go to the bed or to my knees?"

Goddamn, he thought, blowing out a breath. What man didn't want to hear the woman he was attracted to ask a question like that? Unfortunately, it made it difficult to concentrate on the task at hand...

What *was* the task at hand?

When he didn't answer her right away, she must have taken that as a bad sign. Her chocolate brown eyes got that worried look in them again. Although, thankfully, not so bad as before. Maybe Lynne was a bit less anxious around him now—he hoped.

"I guess that's not inventive enough," she whispered. Her teeth sank into her lower lip in the most adorable way. "I guess I'm not really good at this. I can try harder—"

"Lynne," Jesse cut in, his hand absently running over his scarred jaw. He had a task to see to here. Maybe if he turned around and quit lusting after her naked body he could remember what the hell it was. He sighed as he closed his eyes. "You're very good at this," he growled. "Very, very good. But we need to talk..."

His voice trailed off as he got the distinct impression he was the only one having this conversation. His eyes flew open. He grunted when he realized that Lynne had walked off. Frowning, he turned around on his heel to locate her. "I said we need to..."

Jesse swallowed roughly when his gaze found Lynne. She had crawled up onto the bed and gotten herself in the doggy position. Ass up, head down. Holy shit. "...talk," he softly finished.

His jaw clenched as he walked towards the bed. This was too much temptation for any man, let alone one with a high sex drive who had been inside a woman only twice in seven years—and one of those occasions had been this morning. Jesse'd been totally celibate for the past five years simply because there had been no choice in prison, or none he cared to experience anyway. The two years prior to that had been spent with a dark cloud of suspicion hanging over his head, keeping every available woman in Florida, Georgia, and probably all of the USA too wary of him to even consider a date let alone sex. Except for his ex-girlfriend Jeannie. Her he had slept with once.

"I hope this is inventive enough," Lynne whispered, snagging Jesse's attention. "My ex-husband is the only man I've been with besides you," she admitted, "and he preferred having sex with other women instead of me. So, I'm not too good at this."

Her soft voice coupled with her blunt honesty twisted something inside of him. "Your husband was a dick," he growled. "He deserves to have his balls whacked off—"

Jesse stopped mid-sentence when he saw Lynne's body tense. She probably assumed he meant to cut them off himself. Shit. He kept making things worse and worse.

"Well," she said quietly, reflectively. "I think that he probably does."

His eyebrows rose. He found himself amused despite what Lynne thought of him. Little Ms. Docile had just given the big, bad serial rapist permission to whack off her ex's balls. Tiny little Lynne had a mean streak. Who knew?

"Listen," Jesse sighed, finally recalling what the task at hand had initially been. "There are some things about me you really need to know. They affect you. And your future—"

"Oh goodness," Lynne breathed out. She began wiggling her ass in a provocative way that made his cock impossibly harder. "Can't we talk about my future, or lack of it, later?"

He frowned. That wasn't what he'd meant.

With her head still lowered to the bed, she brought her hands around and used her fingers to spread her pussy lips apart. His muscles knotted. "Maybe it's still tight," she said in a hopeful voice. She hoisted her ass up higher, that sexy, hot cunt on full display.

The task at hand was immediately forgotten. Again.

"You're killing me here," he rasped out even as he walked to the bed and palmed the globes of her luscious, round ass. "Fucking killing me."

"Oh I wouldn't be stupid enough to try that," she said with painful honesty. Not because she didn't want to, he thought. Because she was afraid he'd live and retaliate.

She released her pussy lips. Jesse lost his train of thought, mesmerized as he watched the small, slick folds softly close. He took his hands and opened them back up again and simply stared. Goddamn, he loved her cunt.

Lynne put her hands back on the bed so she could recline on her elbows. She tugged at the chain attached to the collar to give herself more leeway, then wiggled her ass again, making his teeth grit. "Do you like to do it this way?" she asked. "I saw it in a movie my husband made me watch and I—"

"Don't," he said probably a bit too roughly, "talk about your ex-husband."

She stilled. "I'm sorry."

Jesse palmed the globes of her ass again, his breathing labored. "I love your body, Lynne. I goddamn love it."

She probably didn't know what to say to that, but it was just as well. Rational thought had once again deserted him. He poised the tip of his swollen cock at the entrance to her pussy. Nostrils flaring, Jesse sank into her tight cunt on a groan, seating himself to the hilt.

"You feel so good," he hoarsely praised her as he began to slowly plunge in and out of her. He closed his eyes and savored the feeling of being inside of her. "So wet and sexy. You're the sexiest woman I've ever met."

"Thank you," she whispered.

"Throw your hips back at me," he ground out. "Squeeze my cock with your tight little cunt."

She did—sweet lord how she did. He'd never felt a pussy this good. Nobody had a wet, suctioning, tight cunt like Lynne.

She threw her hips back at him in frenzied gyrations, not able to stop herself from eliciting a small groan. But neither did he want her to stop. His jaw clenched as he banged away inside of her, grinding his cock as far into her pussy as it could go.

The sound of flesh slapping against flesh echoed in the small cabin. The scent of sex permeated the air. Jesse's fingers found her clit and briskly rubbed it. She moaned in reaction, louder and longer this time. He kept up the steady rubbing motion as he fucked her, wanting her to climax.

"Please," Lynne gasped as she threw her hips back at him. "I think I'm about to do something and I don't know what...oh—I don't like this!"

Jesse's eyes slightly widened as he pumped in and out of her. Didn't she recognize an orgasm when it was coming? If not, her husband was a bigger loser than he'd thought. He rubbed her clit harder, fucked her harder, the sound of her moans making him growl like an animal.

"I won't ever hurt you," he said hoarsely as he sank in and out of her cunt. "It's okay to let go. You're safe."

"I—oh God this feels weird," she gasped.

"Go with it," he gritted out. His jugular bulged as he plunged into her pussy in lightning quick strokes. He rubbed her clit faster, arrogantly pleased when he felt her cunt squeeze in a telling way.

"I—*ohhhhhhh*," Lynne moaned. "*Ohhhhh.*" She threw her hips back at him as she came, her pussy clenching and contracting around his stiff cock.

"Shit," Jesse muttered as he fucked her harder. Her cunt felt so damn good, so tight and inviting. He didn't want this moment to end, but realized he couldn't stave off the inevitable for more than another few seconds. Not with her cunt milking him like that.

Growling low in his throat, he took her faster, violently pumping away inside of her. The sound of her suctioning pussy repeatedly enveloping him was his undoing. "I'm coming," he panted, sinking his cock in and out. "*Here I come...*"

He came on a bellow, his muscles corded and slick with perspiration as he bodily shuddered. He moaned as he spurted, hot cum shooting into her tight cunt as he continued to slam away inside of her. "Lynne," he groaned, loving the way she was throwing her hips back at him to extract all his cum. "Lynne—*shit.*"

When it was over, when Jesse had collapsed on the bed spent and exhausted, they both laid there strangely quiet, her back pressed against his front. It was at least twenty minutes before either of them moved a muscle, let alone spoke.

"Jesse?" Lynne whispered.

His gut clenched. It was the first time she'd ever used his first name. "Yeah?"

"Did you mean what you said? About not hurting me, I mean?"

"Yes," he answered without missing a beat. He sighed. "Lynne, I'm not going to hurt anyone, but especially not you."

She was quiet for a moment. "Thank you," she said softly.

He grunted. "Let's rest a while." He gently squeezed her middle with the muscled arm draped over her. "We'll talk later."

Chapter 5

Lynne watched Jesse wolf down what was left of the beef stew before standing to go heat up another can of it. She felt in a daze from their earlier sexual encounter, her thoughts and emotions in turmoil.

Her very first orgasm. She finally knew what one felt like. It was pretty embarrassing to be thirty-four years old and admit that you've never experienced climax. She had been raised so damn sheltered growing up that masturbation was never a part of her sexual repertoire. She had decided that would change with everything else once she reached Charleston. She should have had her first orgasm there…not here.

Her first climax, she thought. This should have been one of the best nights of her life, but instead she felt embarrassed and ashamed. She had never orgasmed for her husband. She had, however, orgasmed for a serial rapist and killer. Not an easy thing to live with.

As a result, Lynne was torn between anger and disbelief. Anger that her first climax had occurred under horrible conditions. Disbelief that it had occurred at all. Steve had said she was frigid. Apparently she wasn't. Still, she would have preferred to find out that particular piece of information about herself under any circumstances but the one she currently found herself in.

Her nostrils flaring, Lynne carried the pot of beef stew over to the kitchen table where Jesse sat. She dished him out a heaping helping, refusing to make eye contact as she did so.

Jesse's eyebrows slowly drew together. "Thanks," he muttered.

"You're welcome," she crisply replied as she carried the pot back to the stove and set it down with a bang.

Her captor was quiet for a long moment, though she could feel his eyes boring into the back of her. "Care to tell me what's wrong?" he drawled.

Her back stiffened from where she stood in front of the stove. "As if you really care," she bit out. Lynne supposed speaking to him in such a manner wasn't the brightest move she'd ever made, but she was too upset to care. Later, perhaps while he was strangling her, she would regret it. For now it felt damn good.

He grunted. "Tell me what's wrong, Lynne. Don't play games with me."

She whirled around to face him, her long dark hair cascading down one shoulder. She was tired of being scared. She was sick to death of being a victim. All of her life—all of it—if it wasn't one man hurting her it was another. "Why did you do that to me?" she choked out. "Why?"

Jesse's eyes widened almost imperceptibly. He didn't pretend not to know what she was talking about. "I'm sorry," he murmured. "You deserved to have that happen for the first time with any man but me." He sighed, glancing away. "I am sorry. For whatever it's worth."

Lynne blinked, surprised. She had expected him to be angry, not apologetic. Quite frankly, she didn't know how to take the moment. And although she'd never say it aloud, the words were worth a lot. "Thank you," she whispered, confused. She slowly turned back around, her eyes unblinking, to face the stove.

She wasn't certain she was up to more conversation, yet couldn't help but to wonder if this wouldn't be the ideal time to ask the questions she needed answers to. Now, when he seemed in a good enough mood. A million thoughts competing for attention were swimming through her mind. The most prominent one, however, was whether or not he planned to let her leave this cabin—ever. She wanted to ask, but was afraid to. Strangely enough, she wasn't so much scared of Jesse harming her for asking the question to begin with as she was afraid of his answer.

What if he said she could never leave? What then?

"I said we'd talk later," Jesse grumbled. "It's later. Let's talk."

Lynne closed her eyes and took a steadying breath. "What do you want to talk about?" she asked, her back still to him.

"You," he said simply. "I know you must be wondering how long I plan to keep you."

Apparently he was psychic, she thought morosely, her heartbeat accelerating. Yes, she wanted to know. But if his answer was one she didn't want to hear…

She turned around to face him, her eyes wild. "Please," she breathed out. "I don't think I'm ready to talk about this yet."

"Lynne—"

"I was supposed to start a new life," she interrupted. She offered him a shaky smile. "I was driving toward my new life when I crashed into that tree. Now my life is being a naked prisoner wearing a dog collar and chain." She closed her eyes and rubbed her temples. "I don't think I can stand hearing anything more at this point."

His eyes narrowed. "This new life. It involved a man?"

Her eyes flew open. What did that have to do with anything? "A man?" she asked, perplexed as to why the answer seemed so important to him. "No." She slowly shook her head. "I bought my first house. In Charleston. I wanted to build my life somewhere else after the divorce."

That seemed to appease him. "I see," he rumbled out. Silence.

"I didn't kill those girls, Lynne," Jesse said softly, surprising her. Her eyes widened. "I didn't rape them either. I know you won't believe me, which is why I never bothered to say so, but I'm saying it anyway."

It was so quiet she could have heard a pin drop. She was so stunned all she could do was stand there and gape.

She didn't know what to think of Jesse's confession. She wanted to believe him—good God she wanted to believe him!—because it gave her hope where little existed.

Hope that he meant what he'd said, that he'd never harm her. Hope that she would leave here one day alive.

Her gaze raked over his grim masculine features. Even sitting, making no move to touch her, Jesse Redshaw looked like a larger than life vengeful god. The muscles in his arms rippled without doing anything more than moving them. He was big and huge and solid and...well, she was certain he wielded the power to take out another life. But would he was the real question.

"Every man sitting behind bars is innocent according to them," Jesse muttered as he absently ran a hand through his short crew cut. "Hell, I know that. That's one reason I knew nobody would ever believe me. My own goddamn lawyer didn't believe me. So I took matters into my own hands." His voice trailed off into a murmur, his expression far away. "I won't spend the rest of my natural born life behind bars for things I never did, Lynne. I never claimed to be a saint." He shook his head a bit. "But kill a woman? Physically force myself on another person? No. That I can't do."

Her heart was thumping so dramatically it felt like it was ready to beat right out of her chest. She didn't know what to believe. She felt torn. He had saved her life, yes, but he was also holding her against her will. One good deed did not an innocent man make. And yet…

"What happened?" Lynne heard herself softly ask. "If you didn't do it, who did?"

Jesse frowned. His penetrating green gaze found hers. "I don't know. I wish I did. All I know is that it wasn't me."

She didn't say anything else. She didn't know what to say. The silence that followed felt interminable before he spoke again.

Jesse sighed, standing up and pushing himself away from the table. "I have a bondage fetish," he tersely admitted. "Fetish is an ugly word that really means nothing more than something that turns a person on. What turns me on is sexually dominating a woman I'm involved with. No, I more than get turned on by it…I love it, *crave it*."

She nervously averted her gaze.

"From the time I first snuck a dirty magazine from my old man and saw images of women tied up or on their knees submitting to a man, I knew that's what I wanted. I can't explain it any more than I can explain why I'm attracted to brunettes. It just is, if you know what I mean."

Lynne glanced back to where he was standing. Her dark eyes absently raked over his powerful, nude body before finding his face.

Jesse plopped back down in the kitchen chair with a thud. "So when I grew up and developed relationships with women, I went for it. I wasn't discreet about it either. If a woman I was dating wasn't into that, we didn't last long. I enjoy having regular sex too, but on an everyday basis I don't find it all that fulfilling."

Lynne's forehead wrinkled. She didn't exactly understand what this had to do with the issue at hand. His next words, however, shed some more light.

"It's a known fact to every sex crime detective in existence that the majority of sexual predators out there are drawn to bondage. Usually when these guys are arrested, the police confiscate loads of bondage magazines and bondage porn from the offender's house." He frowned. "I was into bondage. I wasn't quiet about it. I resembled the sketch the police artist made. I didn't have an alibi for two of the rapes." He sighed. "The police put two and two together and came up with five."

Lynne drew in a deep breath and slowly expelled it, her thoughts in chaos. She could see where the police would make a correlation like that. She could also see where it might be a faulty one. Like ice-cream and burglaries.

Statistically speaking, one could argue the two are directly correlated because burglaries go up on days ice-cream sales go up. They are related, yes, but one does not cause the other. There is a third variable that comes into play and explains both — heat. Burglaries go up as weather permits the same as ice-cream sales do.

Using that logic, bondage fantasies and sexual offenses were related, but you couldn't argue that someone into bondage would also commit a sexual crime anymore than you could argue all burglars stop off for an ice-cream after stealing a TV.

Still, as much as she wished it otherwise, that didn't make Jesse Redshaw innocent.

"How do you explain the fact there were no related murders after you were imprisoned?" Lynne whispered.

Jesse slowly shook his head. "I can't," he murmured, his gaze snagging hers. "And that's why I didn't stand a chance at getting out." He frowned. "Maybe there were more killings and no bodies have been found yet. Maybe the guy moved on when I got arrested, figuring he better leave the state before the police found out it wasn't me. I don't know, Lynne. I just don't know."

Silence.

He stood up again, pushing away from the table. "I know you don't believe me," he muttered as he walked toward the tiny bedroom a few feet away. "And you don't have to because it's not important."

She sensed that it was, but she said nothing. Her gaze followed him to the empty dresser that hosted nothing but the prison jumpsuit and what was left of the clothes he'd cut off her to check for wounds when she'd been unconscious. She watched him put the jumpsuit on, his back muscles rippling as he bent over.

"I know the big question for you is when the hell you get out of this place. That I still have to figure out," he said as he pulled the faded blue jumpsuit on. "You don't know exactly where here is, but you have a good enough idea. If I let you go, I risk going back to prison which is a risk I don't want to take."

Lynne closed her eyes and took a deep breath. "What if I said I wouldn't turn you in?" she asked. She opened her eyes, watching him pick up the axe he would use to chop up more logs for the fireplace. "What if I promised not to say a word?"

Jesse came to a standstill before her, the large axe resting on one shoulder. "I'd say you know what it feels like to be me."

She shook her head. "I don't understand…"

His gaze found hers and held it. "No matter what you do," he said softly, "and no matter what you say, your words will never be believed."

Her eyes widened as she watched him open the cabin door and walk out into the cold, wintry night.

Chapter 6

The week that followed was an emotionally tumultuous one for Lynne. She was coming to care for her captor and that wouldn't do at all.

Jesse Redshaw was a man who had been convicted of doing some awful things in his life. Things so terrible she couldn't stomach thinking about them. And yet she couldn't deny that feelings for him were quickly developing. She couldn't stop them no matter how hard she tried.

He was kind to her, gentle with her. He was the man who saved her life. The man who'd given her an orgasm for the first time, and many more times after that.

It was hard to reconcile her Jesse to the other Jesse, the one who was supposed to be sitting behind bars on death row in Florida. Of course, according to the man in question, there was nothing to reconcile.

Lynne stood in the kitchen preparing dinner, her gaze occasionally flicking up to the window where she could watch "her" Jesse chop up kindling and logs. As cold as it was outside she saw sweat making his muscles glisten as he repeatedly heaved the huge axe above his head and bore down.

Jesse, she sighed. A total enigma.

Three days ago they had trekked back to where he'd hidden her vehicle under snow and brush. They retrieved her suitcases and various personal items from it, so now at least she had warm clothes. The collar and chain were always on her though. At night, he liked her to sleep nude.

She'd found a few of Steve's old things she hadn't realized were in the SUV, so Jesse didn't have to choose between nudity or the prison jumpsuit anymore. Not that he minded being nude. In fact, it seemed to be his favorite wardrobe given how much of the time he spent wearing it.

One thing was for certain; he loved sex. Lots and lots of sex. Lynne had done it more times in the past week than she'd done it throughout the duration of her marriage to Steve. Every time she turned around, Jesse'd have that look in his eyes. The look that said he'd give anything to be inside of her. She supposed part of it had to do with making up for lost time, though she suspected the major part of it was simply because he liked doing it.

He seemed to revel in all aspects of sex, but she could tell he especially enjoyed performing on her orally. At least once a day, though usually right before bedtime, he would look at her as if to say, *Can I? Please?* The next thing she knew she'd be on her back, gasping and groaning as his mouth enthusiastically sucked on her clit.

Lynne had never told him no to sex, or even tried to tell him no to it. In the beginning her reason had been fear—fear of him becoming angry and hurting her or worse. Now she didn't know anymore.

She wanted to believe she immediately stripped down and gave him blowjobs and sex when his eyes got that heated look in them because he held the upper hand. She wanted to believe it, but didn't know if that view of events was still accurate. It sickened Lynne to think that she could fall in love outside of two weeks—one of which she'd spent unconscious!—with a serial rapist and murderer.

But then Jesse claimed to be innocent.

She didn't want to be one of those people who naïvely believed everything she was told, but neither did she want to be so close-minded as to not open herself up to other possibilities.

A jury had convicted him. But was the jury right?

She recalled enough about the Jesse Redshaw case to remember the fact that blood had been found at only one of the crime scenes...and that it hadn't matched either Jesse or the victim's blood type. Because the tiny stain had been located in the victim's car, the prosecution had explained that away as potentially belonging to anybody who had ridden in her car and sustained a pinprick—it didn't follow that it had to belong to the killer, they had said.

In the end, the man standing outside the kitchen window chopping wood had been sentenced to die on the basis of a scar and a draw toward bondage. Was that enough to make him guilty?

Lynne recalled the social climate in Florida at the time as well. Women were scared. Parents were afraid to let their daughters leave the house. The public wanted a conviction and they wanted it yesterday...

Did it follow that Jesse Redshaw was guilty?

Lynne's teeth sank into her bottom lip. She just didn't know anymore. She didn't want to believe him simply because it made her feel better to, but neither did she want to disbelieve him simply because it was easier than giving him the benefit of doubt.

A scar and bondage. She sighed. It all came down to a scar and bondage.

Lynne had been at the receiving end of Jesse's brand of bondage quite a few times in the past week. He hadn't lied when he'd told her seven days ago that images of female submission made him extremely aroused. She suspected that just looking at the collar she wore made him hot.

He often held her hands above her head while they had sex. Twice, he had asked if he could tie her up. When she had told him no, he had accepted her decision with good grace, never once trying to guilt her into doing something she didn't possess enough trust in him to do. Last night had been one of those times.

His erect penis buried deep inside of her, he gazed down at her through heavy eyelids. "Do you trust me enough yet?" Jesse murmured. He rotated his hips and plunged his stiff cock in a bit deeper.

Lynne gasped before searching his gaze. "I'm not ready. I'm confused about what I feel," she whispered. Her eyes pleaded with him to understand. "My heart believes you, but my head…"

Jesse bent his neck to kiss the tip of her nose before gazing back down at her. "Hey," he said softly, "I'll take whatever you can give." His intense eyes searched hers. "And of the two, I'd rather have your heart anyway."

Something in the vicinity of said heart wrenched. "Thank you for understanding…"

He liked bondage. He loved bondage. Jesse had never lied about that. But inflicting pain on another person? She could honestly say he didn't seem the type to enjoy something like that. She could only recall one time he'd caused her to yelp and that had been an inadvertent elbow to the rib cage when he turned quickly, not realizing she'd walked up behind him.

He had apologized profusely. He had seemed more upset than she was.

Lynne closed her eyes and took a deep breath. This was so damn confusing.

"Hey. You okay?"

Her eyes flew open. She whirled around on her barefoot heel to face him. "I didn't hear you come in," she breathed out.

Jesse stood a couple feet away, his naked torso glistening with perspiration, and stared at her as if trying to guess her thoughts. "You look like you lost your best friend," he said slowly. He set the axe down next to the cabin's front door. "Anything you want to talk about?"

She shook her head, then turned back to face the kitchen window. "I'm just thinking about things is all."

He was quiet for a long moment. "About the rapes you mean?" he asked softly as he walked toward where she was standing.

Lynne shrugged, her back to him. "Yes. That and other things."

Jesse sighed. He said nothing at first, simply placed his hands on her shoulders. "I haven't given you much time to do that, have I? Think, that is." When she didn't say anything, he squeezed her shoulders to let her know it was okay. "Take all the time you need, Lynne. I'll be here when you figure things out."

Her forehead wrinkled. "What do you mean?"

"I shouldn't be pushing you for sex," he murmured. "Not until you know for sure that you want to have it with me."

"You've never pushed me," she whispered. "It's not about that. It's just that I'm so damn...confused," she admitted.

Silence.

"At least you're thinking about it," he decided. "That's more decency than anyone else has shown me."

Lynne's shoulders slumped. "I'm sorry I—"

"Don't be," Jesse cut in. "You'd be stupid not to be skeptical." He squeezed her shoulders again, then walked away to clean himself up. "Take all the time you need."

Chapter 7
Two nights later...

Jesse woke up in the middle of the night with a painful erection. Lying on his back, his hands propped behind his head, he blew out a breath as he and his cock stared at the ceiling.

He hadn't made a move to touch Lynne in two days. It was the right thing to do, he consoled himself. It was the right thing to do, but the most difficult as well. Just thinking about her tight, suctioning cunt made him hard as a rock. And those nipples...

He frowned, telling himself not to go there.

One good thing had come of the past two sexless days, however. Even if she didn't believe him about the rapes, he was fairly certain Lynne believed he wouldn't harm her in particular. That was a good thing. A nice start.

The bad part was he doubted sexy little Lynne would start anticipating his sexual needs again like she used to, especially now that the fear of being hacked up into a million pieces was gone. He grimly conceded that he almost wished he'd let her live with her damn illusions.

But that wouldn't have been right. Mentally, she had gone through enough already and he didn't want to take her through more.

Jesse realized that Lynne was dealing with more than just questions about his past and whether or not he could be believed. She was also dealing with the reality of the moment, the reality of her confinement. He knew she didn't want to be forced to stay in the cabin with him. The thing she didn't get was that he didn't want to keep her here against her will, either. He wanted her to stay all right, but he wanted her to stay because she wanted to—something he knew would never happen.

Caring for her all of those days, not knowing if she would live or die, had done something to him on the inside. For years he'd allowed himself to feel nothing for anyone—not since the day when Jeannie had showed up during visitation at the county jail and told him they were over. She didn't believe him, she had said. He looked too much like the guy in the sketch, she had said. She wouldn't testify on his behalf, wouldn't accept his phone calls—nothing. They were over.

Watching Jeannie walk away had felt like a knife in the gut. If she didn't believe him, he held little hope that anyone else would. And, of course, he had been right. Nobody had believed him then and nobody believed him now.

After that Jesse had closed himself off entirely. It wasn't like it mattered anyway. In prison there was no one to get close to unless you like your bread buttered up the ass, which he didn't. Closing himself off had been easy. Until he met Lynne.

By the time he'd gotten her out of the banged-up SUV, she had already been unconscious. Her head had taken a pretty serious hit and, given the gash in it, he suspected from more than just the airbag. He hadn't thought she would live past the night, but she did. He'd taken good care of her, watched her as vigilantly as a guard dog, had only left her side long enough to bow-hunt for food and chop wood for the fireplace.

Two days later, she started coming-to in short, brief spells. He doubted Lynne would remember much of it, if anything at all, because the fever had kept her half delirious. She hadn't become cognizant of her surroundings until the fifth day.

Jesse was thankful she couldn't recall those first few days because he was pretty sure Lynne would think even less of him — assuming that was possible — if she knew he'd touched her intimately. He hadn't penetrated her or anything like that, but he had sucked on her nipples. A pretty shitty thing to do to an unconscious woman, he realized. There were no excuses for it. The only thing he could even say in his defense was that he had felt such tender emotions toward her when he'd been caring for her, and it had been a really long time since he'd been close to a naked woman, and her nipples were so stiff and —

He sighed. There weren't any excuses. Of all the things for a convicted rapist proclaiming his innocence to do that had to have been about the dumbest choice he'd made yet.

Jesse laid in the bed, his swollen penis throbbing for release, but he didn't touch himself. He wouldn't masturbate with Lynne lying right next to him because it seemed disrespectful somehow. Plus, he thought grimly, he wanted *her*. Not his hand. He'd had enough of his hand in prison to last a lifetime.

Shit, he needed release, Jesse thought as he got up out of the bed, his teeth gritting. He was so goddamn hard it ached.

Being as quiet as he could, he stalked off toward the cabin's tiny kitchen and ran himself a glass of water from the sink. He gulped it down quickly, the cool liquid soothing his dry throat. Unfortunately it didn't do anything toward quelling his raging hard-on.

"Jesse?" he heard Lynne softly call out. Her voice was groggy with sleep. "Is everything okay?"

He sighed. "Yeah. Go back to sleep," he muttered. When he turned around, however, he saw that she was sitting up. Her eyes widened a bit when she saw his erection. He frowned, turning back around to face the sink. "Go to sleep, Lynne."

It was quiet for a long moment; so long in fact that he thought she'd heeded his advice. He was surprised when he heard her delicately clear her throat, announcing the fact she was standing behind him without saying the words. Jesse cocked his head, looking at her from over his shoulder.

She blushed a bit, glancing away before she slowly met his gaze. "What would you like?" she quietly asked. "Should I go to the bed or to my knees?"

His hard-on started throbbing again. He blew out a breath, then turned to stare out the window. "I told you I wouldn't hurt you, Lynne," he murmured. "You don't have to have sex with me to stay on my good side. You've been on it since the moment I laid eyes on you."

Silence.

"What would you like?" Lynne whispered. "Should I go to the bed or to my knees?"

Jesse stilled. His head slowly came around until he could stare at her. His intense green gaze raked over her body. "The bed," he said hoarsely.

Lynne nodded. She turned around and walked back to the bed, then climbed up on it and laid down on her back. She spread her thighs wide, waiting for him. "Do you think..." She smiled a bit nervously. "Maybe you could do, *you-know-what*, to me again?"

He bodily turned around to face her, his penis standing stiff up against his navel. She tended to be so genteel in her language she even had a difficult time asking him to eat her out. Nobody but nobody got him hard like Lynne.

"You're killing me here," he said thickly as he slowly strode toward the bed. "You're goddamn killing me."

Half afraid she'd change her mind and half just wanting to touch her, Jesse moved to his knees in a lightning quick motion, then dove face first for her pussy to do *you-know-what*. She gasped, just like she always did. He groaned from around her hole, covering it with his mouth and vigorously sucking it.

"Oh wow," Lynne breathed out. Her hips reared up a bit, offering him better access to her flesh. His nostrils flared as he sucked harder.

Jesse used his hands to spread apart her pussy lips then wrapped his warm mouth around her clit. She moaned loudly as he sucked on it, her legs shaking, already close to coming.

"Oh," she gasped, her head falling back. She grabbed at his head, running her fingers through his hair, pressing his face closer to her pussy. She groaned as he sucked, the sound arousing him, making him growl against her clit.

Her reaction to his touch made him hope she'd want to stay with him. He knew it would never happen, but nobody said dreams were realistic.

"*Jesse*," Lynne gutturally moaned. Her thighs tellingly trembled from either side of his head. He growled into her pussy as he mercilessly sucked her clit.

"*Oh my God!*" she wailed, her entire body convulsing as she came for him. "*Oh my God! Oh my God!*"

By the time she finished coming, his breathing was so labored he felt dizzy. Goddamn, but she was the sexiest woman he'd ever clapped eyes on. He stood up slowly, towering over Lynne from where she lay on the bed, his penis stiff and wanting her. She looked at him questioningly, as if wondering why he hadn't mounted her yet.

His grim features intensely regarded her. "Are you sure you want me?" he rasped out. "Tell me now because I won't be able to stop once I climb on top of you."

The emotion in his voice was raw. With hope. With lust. With...vulnerability.

Lynne swallowed hard. She knew he was referring to more than sex. He was referring to everything.

"I want you," she whispered. "I'm sure."

She was sure. Nothing had ever felt more certain. She knew Jesse. And what's more, she believed in him. Others might think she was foolish, but she didn't care. Her decision had been made. She chose to place her faith in the only man who had ever shown her nothing but gentleness, kindness, and caring—Jesse Redshaw.

His green eyes were so intense that if she hadn't known him it might have frightened her. He came down on top of her, his big muscular body covering hers. He settled himself between her thighs as he used his callused hand to direct the head of his stiff penis toward her waiting flesh.

"I've missed you," he said thickly, his eyes heavy-lidded.

"I've missed you, too." She smiled softly, running her hands up his hard, chiseled chest and roping them around his neck.

"Do you trust me yet, Lynne?" he murmured.

Her eyes searched his. "I do—I really do." She knew what he wanted. And she was ready to give it to him.

A bit frightened but mostly nervous with excitement, Lynne released her hold from around his neck and tellingly placed her arms over her head.

Jesse stilled. "You're sure, sweetheart?" he hoarsely asked. She could feel his pre-ejaculate wetting the labial fold his penis was thrust up against.

She nodded. Her heart was thumping like crazy, but she realized she wanted to do this for him. It was more than a sexual act. It symbolized total faith in her belief that he'd never harm her—or anyone else. "Completely. I'm ready, Jesse."

He blew out a breath. "I've never been so hard in my life."

It took him all of ten seconds to retrieve some rope and two t-shirts. He wound one shirt around each wrist for padding, then roped and tied them to two bedposts. The look in his eyes when he came down on top of her again was domineering, but loving. Lynne could well imagine how she looked to him—she was the embodiment of every submissive female fantasy he'd envisioned since he'd been old enough to think of such things...

A dog collar and chain was clasped around her neck, her hands were tied above her head to the posts so she couldn't move. The position she'd been bound in caused her breasts to thrust up like two offerings, her nipples standing stiff with arousal.

Jesse lowered his face to her chest on a groan, his hands cupping her breasts together so he could suck both nipples simultaneously. She moaned softly in reaction, her eyelids drifting shut, the pleasure she felt somehow heightened by her lack of mobility.

"Oh wow," she breathed out. She wanted him to suck harder. She lifted her chest up as best she could to let him know that without words. "Jes—Master—that feels so good," she whispered.

He sucked on them harder, a low growl in the back of his throat as he toyed with them. He relentlessly sucked on them until they were swollen and stiff, until Lynne was gasping and groaning and wanting to be fucked.

Jesse raised his head, the sound of nipples popping from his mouth making her eyes open. He grinned down at her. "You remembered the Master bit from one of our talks, eh?"

She grinned back. "I kind of like it," she admitted, blushing just a bit.

His expression turned serious, his eyes getting that glazed-over, heated look in them again. "I love it," he murmured. "Call me that anytime."

His nostrils flaring, he settled himself between her cushiony thighs again, then pushed the head of his thick cock inside of her. Her breath caught in the back of her throat. "Your pussy is always so tight," he rasped. "Goddamn, you feel good, Lynne."

Jesse sucked in his breath as he began to slowly sink his cock in and out of her body. She moaned, her head falling back into the pillows, her breasts thrusting up again. The sound of her wet flesh suctioning him back in on every outstroke aroused her just as it always did.

"Jesse," she whispered. "Mmmmm."

"Mmmm is right," he said thickly. He bent his neck and licked her nipples, teasing them with teeth and tongue. "I love your tits," he mumbled from around one.

He picked up the pace of his pumping, plunging his cock in and out of her in faster, deeper strokes. Raising his head from her breasts, his teeth gritted and perspiration dotted his brow. "I love your cunt," he ground out, riding her harder. "I love *you*, Lynne."

Her eyes widened. "Oh Jesse—"

She might have said more, but he took her hard then, thrusting in and out of her in animalistic strokes. Lynne groaned, her legs instinctively wrapping around his hips to hold on while he rode her.

"I love you so much, Lynne," he panted before his lips came down to find hers. "So goddamn much."

Jesse covered her lips with his in what was to be their first kiss. His tongue thrust inside, sweeping against hers as he slanted his mouth this way and that over hers. She kissed him back enthusiastically, groaning into his mouth as he made love to her. They were intimate like that for long moments, enjoying the taste and feel of the other.

"Fuck me," Lynne gasped, pulling her mouth away from his, wanting to feel him orgasm inside of her. She knew those words would arouse him. She knew everything that aroused him. "Please, Master," she begged. "It makes me feel close to you."

Jesse's nostrils flared. He stopped thrusting long enough to come up to his knees and throw her legs over his shoulders. He plunged into her in a long, smooth stroke, her head falling back on a groan.

"Like this?" he ground out, grinding his cock into her. He rotated his hips, pistoning back and forth in fast, deep strokes. His jaw clenched as he fucked her hard, plunging in and out of her pussy like he meant to brand it. The sound of her flesh suctioning him back in echoed throughout the cabin, competing with the sound of her moaning. Unable to move her upper body, she laid there and took everything he had to give, wanting him to mate with her as hard and deep as humanly possible.

"Goddamn, I love your cunt," he said hoarsely, his eyes shuttering as he sank his stiff cock inside of her, over and over, again and again.

"Jesse," she gasped. The friction on her clit in this position was too much. She groaned, her eyes closing as her body prepared to come.

"Do it, baby," he ground out, fucking her faster, harder, deeper. "I love making you come."

Lynne moaned like a wounded animal, her nipples stabbing up into the air as she came. "*Oh God,*" she groaned, her head thrashing back and forth. Her face felt hot, her nipples painfully swollen. Not being able to move only added to it. "*Jesse.*"

Jesse took her legs from off his shoulders and came down on top of her again without missing a beat. His nostrils flared as he mounted her hard, pounding in and out of her pussy in branding strokes. "My cunt," he growled. "All mine."

"*Yes!*" she screamed, her muscles tensing as she climaxed again. "*Oh God!*"

His muscles tensed as he possessively fucked her. He closed his eyes and gritted his teeth as he repeatedly sank into her, letting Lynne know he wanted to prolong the moment, but couldn't.

"I'm coming," he said hoarsely, one callused hand wrapping around a fistful of her long, dark hair. He held onto it tightly, his jaw clenching as he plunged into her pussy once, twice, three times more. "*Lynne,*" he gasped, his entire body shuddering atop hers. He groaned long and loud as he spurt his hot cum inside of her, his cock still violently pumping away as her cunt milked him, extracting all of his seed.

"Shit," he rasped, bringing his strokes down in pace. His breathing was heavy, his words coming out in a long mumble. "That was the best sex ever in the history of best sex."

Lynne smiled, pleased she'd made him feel that way, but said nothing.

When it was over, Jesse didn't move for a long moment. He simply laid there on top of her, hugging her body close to his. He didn't seem as though he wanted to untie her, but eventually he reached up and unwound the knots with one hand.

Lynne smiled contentedly, no longer afraid to admit to herself—or him—how she felt. "I love you," she whispered, her unbound hands running over his chiseled back. "Very much."

He came up on his elbows and stared down at her, his heart in his eyes. "Ah Lynne. I love you, too." He briefly closed his eyes and sighed, the defeated expression on his face causing her smile to fade.

"What is it?" she quietly asked, worry tinting the question.

Silence.

"Jesse?" she murmured.

"I can't do this," he said softly, coming up from his elbows. He stood up then turned away from her, his hands on his hips in a football player's stance. "I can't take a gift like that from you, say I love you, and then make you stay here. It's not right."

Lynne shot up into a sitting position. Her eyes went wide. "Jesse, don't say that," she pleaded in a small voice. "I don't want to leave here without you."

He cocked his head to stare at her. His smile was sad. "Do you know how many times I've fantasized about hearing you say those very words?" he murmured. He shook his head and glanced away. "I never thought I'd let you go if you said them to me, but now that you did I know I have to."

She felt like she was going to be sick. "You don't want me anymore?"

He turned around to face her, his green gaze intense. "Lady, I want you more than I've ever wanted anyone in my entire life."

"Then why are you doing this?" she shakily asked.

"Because if you ever come back to me I want it to be for the right reasons." Jesse forced a smile to his lips. "Come on, Lynne. I'll help you get that SUV of yours running again." He took a deep breath, then held out a hand to her. "Your folks are worried. You have things you need to do."

Lynne's heart felt like it might break. She missed her family, and he was right, she knew they must be sick with grief. But she didn't want to leave Jesse either. She took his hand with misgivings, hesitantly accepting his help off of the bed.

She stood before him, her eyes searching his. "What if I decide to come back?" she asked, her voice catching.

Jesse stilled. Something in his expression told her he knew that would never happen, that once she got back to reality she'd forget about the man in the remote West Virginia cabin. And yet, despite that, he was letting her go anyway.

Because he loved her.

"You'd make me the happiest man on earth," he murmured.

His gaze gentled, the expression on his face resolved and accepting. "I want you to be happy, Lynne. You deserve it." She could have sworn she saw a trace of a tear in the corner of his eye, but decided she might have been imagining that. "Go to Charleston and start that new life," he whispered. "You never know where it might lead."

Chapter 8
Three months later…

Leaving the tiny cabin on the snowy, remote West Virginia mountaintop had been the most difficult choice Lynne had ever made. And yet, it had also been the most freeing. It meant that life was up to her now, the future whichever one she chose to create.

Jesse had let her leave him three months ago. She knew he hadn't wanted to, but neither had he wanted her to be unhappy. Unlike him, she had a life waiting for her somewhere else, friends and relatives she knew were worried sick wondering if she was dead or alive.

It had been a good three months. Seeing the people she loved again had been wonderful. She'd cried and cried when her mother wept as she threw her arms around her. She'd explained her disappearance away to everyone's satisfaction, claiming she'd had amnesia for a couple of weeks after she'd woken up from the accident.

Working at home was good. Her house in Charleston was a dream come true. Her new life had turned out just as she'd wanted it to be.

Except for one thing. She missed Jesse. A lot.

Lynne Temple shut the door to her new black SUV and began the long hike that would take her to the tiny, remote cabin…and to the man she loved.

She was nervous about seeing him again, mostly because she feared he'd used the last three months to put her from his mind. She couldn't think of anything that would hurt worse. Especially since he'd been in the forefront of her thoughts night and day.

It was another hour before she came to the well-hidden trail that led to the cabin. It looked a bit different covered with green grass and blossoming flowers instead of snow and ice, but she'd know the trail anywhere.

Throwing her purse over her shoulder, Lynne stealthily made her way up the final incline that would take her to the cabin. Her heart began thumping wildly in her chest when she saw it, nerves and excitement mingling together.

And then she saw him, Jesse, and her heart began racing impossibly faster. He was even bigger and more handsome than he'd been since the last time she'd seen him, all rippling muscles and imposing stance. His crew cut had grown out some, she noticed. His light brown hair was almost collar-length now.

He looked so alone standing in the garden tending to his early spring vegetables that it made her heart squeeze painfully. He deserved more than this, she knew. He deserved to have a life.

"Jesse," she whispered as she came up behind him.

His head snapped around. His eyes widened. "Lynne?" he quietly asked, his expression stunned.

Her eyes softened. His face looked so haggard, so tired.

So lonely.

She smiled tremulously. "I've missed you so much," she breathed out, tears that didn't fall stinging her eyes. "I couldn't stand to be away from you for another day."

Jesse searched her gaze. His expression was surprised, hopeful. "I've missed you, too," he murmured. His eyes lit up. "I don't know how long you plan to visit, but I'm glad you're here."

"I won't be staying long," she informed him.

He nodded, his expression sad but accepting.

"Just long enough," she whispered, "to help you collect your things and take you to Charleston with me. If you choose to stay with me, that is."

He reached out to stroke her face. "I love you, Lynne," he said softly. "I love you more than I've ever loved anyone or anything, but you know I can't leave this mountain."

"I disagree," she said shakily. "Oh ye of little faith."

His forehead wrinkled. "Lynne, I trust you with my whole heart. You know that."

"Then just what do you think I've been doing these past three months?" She smiled at his confused expression, then pulled her purse off of her shoulder and began rifling through the contents. "'Hell hath no fury like a woman scorned.'" Her eyebrows shot up as she handed him a newspaper. "Or a woman unjustly separated from the man she loves."

Jesse slowly withdrew the newspaper from her hand. His gaze flicked from her face down to the headline. He stilled. His eyes widened in disbelief. "Is this for real?" he asked, his tone stunned.

"Oh yeah," Lynne whispered. She smiled, beaming from ear to ear. "Very real."

He was too shocked to do anything but stare at her. She couldn't blame him. Jesse'd gone from being a wanted death row fugitive to a free man in the blink of an eye.

The paper told all about how she'd hired private detectives and used her computer background to do some of her own investigative work, all with the hope of finding enough holes in the "evidence" to at least get Jesse a new trial with a real lawyer representing him. She'd had to tell her family the truth of what happened when the story came out, of course. All of them had been shocked, to say the least. Stunned, but supportive. Her mother had been the first to shoo her off to the cabin, insisting she go get Jesse and bring him back.

The payoff on her hard work and spent money had been better than she ever anticipated. The real rapist had been caught. What's more, his blood was a positive match to the bloodstain found in the first victim's car. Yesterday the killer with a scarred jaw so much like Jesse's had entered a not guilty by reason of insanity plea. Whatever the outcome, Jesse Redshaw was a free man.

"You did this...for me?" he murmured.

Lynne nodded. "I wish I could say your freedom is all due to my brilliance and persistence, but..." She sighed, her smile sad. "You were right about him moving on, Jesse," she whispered. "Police in South Carolina found four more bodies two months ago. At first they thought it was you since you were on the loose, so to speak, but the coroner came back and said it wasn't possible, that the deaths had occurred during a time frame before you had escaped."

"I'm sorry it happened that way," he quietly commiserated.

"Me too." Her dark gaze found his. "But I'm so very glad you're free."

"Ah, Lynne." Jesse picked her up off her feet and gave her a big bear hug. He closed his eyes as he held her, slowly rocking back and forth on his heels. "Thank you," he said a bit shakily. "This is the most incredible thing another person's ever done for me."

She hugged him back tightly, reveling in the feel of his hard body holding hers, breathing in the masculine scent that belonged only to him. "You are welcome," she whispered.

Jesse blinked, then blew out a breath. He squeezed her again before setting her down on her feet. "This feels, well, strange to say the least."

Lynne's teeth sank into her bottom lip.

He raised an eyebrow. "What's wrong?"

"I was just wondering…" She cleared her throat, then spoke a bit louder. "I was wondering where you'll go now that you can go anywhere you want." She blushed as she glanced away.

Jesse palmed either side of her face and forced her to look at him. His green eyes were more intense than she'd ever before seen them. "Lady, you couldn't get rid of me now if you tried."

Lynne took a deep breath to keep from crying. "Promises, promises," she said on a smile.

He didn't smile back. His eyes shone, though. "I think Charleston sounds like a great place to start over again."

"It is," she whispered. Her eyes searched his. "So, are you gonna kiss me or what?"

Jesse grinned. "Kiss you. Marry you. Get brats on you." His eyebrows rose as he drew her into his side and began walking with her down the hill. "I told you, lady, you're never getting rid of me now."

Lynne smiled up to him. The brats part, or at least one brat, was taken care of already. She held back a knowing grin, deciding to tell him later. Lord knows he was dealing with enough shocks right now as it was.

She'd never felt happier or more at peace—or more sure of her future—in her entire life. Her destiny lay with Jesse Redshaw. The man she loved so much it hurt. "Don't you want to get your things before we hike to my car?"

He stilled. They both stopped and turned around to look one last time at the tiny, remote cabin perched in the mountains. The cabin with bittersweet memories. They'd fallen in love there, but they'd both been imprisoned there, too.

Jesse slowly shook his head. He squeezed Lynne closer against him and resumed walking down the incline. "I've got everything I need right here." He bent his neck and kissed the top of her head. "Now take me home so I can tie you up properly."

Lynne chuckled. "Only if you promise to do *you-know-what* to me first."

"Sweetheart," Jesse drawled in that sexy accent of his, "I'll be doing *you-know-what* to you every day for the rest of your life."

"Promises, promises."

Jaid Black

VANISHED

An Ellora's Cave Publication

About the author

Critically acclaimed and highly prolific, Jaid Black is the best-selling author of numerous erotic romance and erotic thriller tales. Her first title, *The Empress' New Clothes*, was recognized as a readers' favorite in women's erotica by Romantic Times magazine and consistently appears on best-selling lists years after its initial publication.

A full-time novelist, Jaid calls herself "a spinner of fantasies—not a documenter of realities." Known for being an "edge" writer, her work often delves into the darkest realms of female sexual fantasies and brings them to light. She currently writes for Ellora's Cave, Pocketbooks (Simon & Schuster), and Berkley/Jove (Penguin Group).

Jaid lives in a cozy little village in the northeastern United States with her two children. In her spare time, she enjoys traveling, shopping, and furthering her collection of African and Egyptian art. She welcomes mail from readers. You can visit her on the web at www.jaidblack.com or write to her at P.O. Box 362, Munroe Falls, OH 44262.

Other Ellora's Cave titles by Jaid Black

Multiple Author Anthologies

- "Devilish Dot" in *Manaconda* (Trek series)
- "Dementia" in *Taken* (Trek series)
- "Death Row: The Mastering" in *Enchained* (Death Row serial)
- "Besieged" in *The Hunted*
- "God of Fire" in *Warrior*
- "Sins of the Father" in *Ties That Bind*

Trek Mi Q'an Series – single titles

- *The Empress' New Clothes*
- *No Mercy*
- *Enslaved*
- "No Escape" & "No Fear" in *Conquest*
- *Seized*

Other single titles

- "Death Row: The Fugitive", "Death Row: The Hunter", & "Death Row: The Avenger" in *Death Row: The Trilogy*
- *The Possession*

Other novellas

- "Warlord"

- "Naughty Nancy" (Trek series)
- "Politically Incorrect – Tale 1: Stalked"

Why an electronic book?

We live in the Information Age — an exciting time in the history of human civilization in which technology rules supreme and continues to progress in leaps and bounds every minute of every hour of every day. For a multitude of reasons, more and more avid literary fans are opting to purchase e-books instead of paperbacks. The question to those not yet initiated to the world of electronic reading is simply: why?

1. *Price.* An electronic title at Ellora's Cave Publishing runs anywhere from 40-75% less than the cover price of the <u>exact same title</u> in paperback format. Why? Cold mathematics. It is less expensive to publish an e-book than it is to publish a paperback, so the savings are passed along to the consumer.

2. *Space.* Running out of room to house your paperback books? That is one worry you will never have with electronic novels. For a low, one-time cost, you can purchase a handheld computer designed specifically for e-reading purposes. Many e-readers are larger than the average handheld, giving you plenty of screen room. Better yet, hundreds of titles can be stored within your new library — a single microchip. (Please note that Ellora's Cave does not endorse any specific brands at this time. You can check our website at www.ellorascave.com under "New To E-Books?" for customer recommendations we make available to new consumers.)

3. *Mobility.* Because your new library now consists of only a microchip, your entire cache of books can be taken with you wherever you go.

4. *Personal preferences are accounted for.* Are the words you are currently reading too small? Too large? Too...**ANNOYING**? Paperback books cannot be modified according to personal preferences, but e-books can.

5. *Innovation.* The way you read a book is not the only advancement the Information Age has gifted the literary community with. There is also the factor of *what* you can read. Ellora's Cave Publishing will be introducing a new line of interactive titles that are available in e-book format only.

6. *Instant gratification.* Is it the middle of the night and all the bookstores are closed? Are you tired of waiting days—sometimes weeks—for online and offline bookstores to ship the novels you bought? Ellora's Cave Publishing sells instantaneous downloads 24 hours a day, 7 days a week, 365 days a year. Our secure e-book delivery system is 100% automated, meaning your order is filled as soon as you pay for it.

Those are a few of the top reasons why electronic novels are displacing paperbacks for many an avid reader. As always, Ellora's Cave Publishing welcomes your questions and comments. We invite you to email us at service@ellorascave.com or write to us directly at: 1337 Commerce Dr. #13, Stow, OH 44224.

Printed in the United States
87616LV00002B/112-402/A